Passages of Peculiarity II

A Collection of Dark Tales

Mark K. McClain

Passages of Peculiarity II by Mark K. McClain

Copyright © 2025 by Mark K. McClain

ISBN

979-8-9892944-5-9 (print)

979-8-9892944-4-2 (ebook)

Published by Next Journey Books (www.nextjourneybooks.com)

Trigger Warning: This book contains mature and potentially distressing content, including—but not limited to—sexual situations, death, strong language, substance use/abuse, murder, and slander of organized religions. Reader discretion is advised. If you find such topics upsetting, please refrain from reading further.

Acknowledgements

For Rochelle

Editor: Lisa Wong
Proofreader: Stefani Evers
Exterior Design: Debbi Stocco

Also by Mark K. McClain

Author's Website

www.nextjourneybooks.com

Introduction

Welcome back, reader. Passages of Peculiarity II drags you deeper into the shadows where waking terror awaits and nightmares breathe. Inside, you will face murder, revenge, twisted monsters, and unnatural horrors dwelling just beyond reason.

Each story is a step into darkness, a brush with madness, a choice between ruin and revelation. But do not expect redemption, only the chance to confront what you would rather leave buried. Here, you will find no solace.

Hateful House

Today, I was hurriedly contacted to see to the welfare of poor Mrs. Wilkinson. Her servants have gone off to their merriments for the Yuletide, leaving her behind in the silence of that great and draft-ridden house—the house many fear.

In the end, I was the only one willing to help the old woman until her staff returns. I may even spread cheer by taking along decorations to show both her and the house some love during my visit. Unfortunately, many believe the structure to be evil or hateful. I say, nonsense. What an utterly silly concept. I have no qualms about going there.

So, while my own children await my return by suppertime, their small faces no doubt pressed to frosted panes in hopeful vigil, I will do what needs done so we may begin their favorite season in earnest.

Before the clock struck noon, with the chill wind biting at even the tiniest bit of exposed flesh, I retrieved the old iron key hidden beneath the withered flowerpot. With a turn of the lock and a groan of hinges, I gained entry into the silence within.

Despite her being a widow of delicate constitution, the old woman keeps this grand house of melancholy solitude in immaculate order.

I had intended only to remain long enough to prepare a simple supper for my charge and see her safely to bed before taking my leave into the encroaching dusk. After all, my own family was waiting for my return.

Yet now, as I pass from room to cavernous room within this echoing mansion, a chill of unease stirs in my bosom. Mrs. Wilkinson is nowhere to be found. The hearth lies cold, the upper halls are cloaked in deep shadow. I call her name, gently at first, then with rising urgency. Yet only silence returns. The house yields no sign of her, only the slow creak of floorboards and the whisper of wind through ill-fitted shutters.

Then it strikes me—subtly at first, like a misstep on an uneven sidewalk—when I cross the threshold of a door on the second floor, I find myself emerging, inexplicably, near the sitting room on the first.

A mistake, surely. I blame some trick of direction, a lapse of memory or attention. But the pattern continues. Repeatedly, I pass through doors—bedchamber, linen closet, study—and each time, the house defies logic. Rooms lead not to their neighbors or outdoors, but to places I have already been, as though the house itself has folded in upon its own bones.

No matter the door I choose, I am always returned to where I began—a strange loop of corridors and turning halls, familiar yet subtly wrong. The air grows colder, the walls seem to lean inward, and my confusion is no longer merely frustrating, but creeping and dreadful.

Growing panic stirs in my bosom, rising like smoke up a chimney. I rush to the nearest window and tear back the heavy, time-stiffened curtains, grasping for any sign of the outside world—of reality.

Beyond the glass, the fields lie blanketed in snow, glittering faintly beneath a pewter sky. I see families at play, children shrieking with laughter as they tumble from sleds, mothers tossing snowballs, fathers hauling wooden toboggans uphill. The world is alive, innocent and untouched.

I cry out, pressing my face to the cold pane, my voice loud, pleading.

"Help! Can you hear me? I am stuck! Help me, *please!*" I place extra emphasis on the last word, but not a soul turns. No one looks. My voice is swallowed by the thick silence within, as if the house is mocking me. Am I invisible?

Anger and frustration take me. I seize the window frame, trying to wrench it open, but it remains unmoving, sealed as though by rusted iron and frost. I strike it with my fists, once, twice, thrice—but it will not yield. Only the dull thud of flesh against glass answers me, and the bitter cold seeping through reminds me: I am here. I am alone.

Thoughts of my children flood my mind again, their little hands reaching for me, laughter at the dinner table, the way the light pools around them near the hearth. Do they wonder where I have gone? Has my husband, steady and practical, begun to question the ticking clock, the lateness of my return? Perhaps even now he searches the lanes, calling my name through the falling snow.

His image kindles a flicker of hope, small, warm, and stubborn. I cradle it for a moment, daring to believe. But as I turn and step once more through a familiar door, I find myself, again, back in the same corridor, the same faded runner beneath my feet, the same gaslight sconce flickering with its sickly glow.

My hope withers. The house, this accursed house, will not let me go. I am trapped. Time, that treacherous warden of sense, is but a forsaken relic here, absent in whole and form.

There is no mortal measure by which I might discern how long I have wandered these accursed passageways. Minutes? Hours? Days? I know not.

Hunger bites at my innards with cruel insistence and thirst sets fire to my throat. My mind, once sharp, is now shrouded in a permeable haze of terror and unrest. Most harrowing of all are the surreal visions of my slow, agonizing demise. Shall I die here within these oak-paneled halls, I wonder?

Too, there is a knocking. Incessant. Perverse. Ever it dogs my steps, a specter bound not by flesh but sound. Four raps, deliberate and slow, each one a tolling bell for my sanity. At times, the sound issues from some far-off recess, like a foul memory long buried but never forgotten. Other times, they erupt just behind me, so close I can scarce restrain a scream as my heart nearly arrests in dreadful anticipation of the next.

No soul ought to bear such torment. Since my arrival, I have known nothing but dread. The lady is nowhere to be found, while doors yield or resist with minds of their own, opening with groans of age and closing without cause. Mocking laughter or desperate echoes of weeping reverberate through the corridors, following, teasing, galling me. The structure itself seems to carry hidden hate.

Even the walls betray reason as doors routinely shift, hurriedly appearing where none stood mere moments earlier. Often, as quickly as they materialize, they vanish from sight. Try as I might, I cannot reach them in what time I have considering my weakened state. Will one lead outside? I can only hope and dream for such relief.

As I pass over the solid wooden floors, my heels clacking softly against the polished planks, a door opens wide with a terrible cry of rusted hinges, as though the house itself drew breath to speak or as if anguishing in pain. I rush toward it in blind panic, hoping the threshold will reveal a means of escape from this nightmarish deception. But it was not to be as the thick wood slams shut ere I reach it.

Tugging and pulling upon the handle avail me naught. Finally, spent in spirit and sore of limb, I abandon the effort. Yet in that very moment, the same door yawns open, revealing naught but a wall of cold, unyielding brick. I stare in disbelief. Another cruel jest from some unseen, spiteful hand.

Is this perversity to be my tomb? Am I meant to slowly fade from existence, until I am naught but a whisper in the shadows, a mere memory fading from the minds of those who once might have known me?

No woman, least of all one guilty only of compassion, should suffer so vile a fate. Is this the lofty toll for living in righteousness? I have endeavored to bring forth good unto this forsaken world. I have wrought no harm, betrayed no trust, nor sullied my speech or deeds. Yet, lo! I am assailed by a malice so vile, its nature I can barely grasp.

My heart sinks lower with each step as my strength wanes more permanently. Heaviness of limb and eyelid slow me in every respect. Thinking has become a chore.

Slowly, I sink to the floor, my will broken as glass crushed beneath a cruel heel. My thoughts lie scattered, a maze of shadows and ruin of my former happy life. My flesh, long denied the balm of rest and sustenance, can persevere no more.

Here shall I perish, remaining ever blind of my transgressions, never to know what sin cast me from the light. I depart this world with no taste of joy's return, no whisper of happiness to bid me farewell. Shall any soul mourn my passing? I cannot know, and the answer shall never grace my ears.

Leaning against the mocking, cruel door, my head tilts to the side, drawn there by despair and ruin of my will. The knocking sound—constant, dreadful—draws ever nearer with each breath, hammering upon my sanity. And just ere madness

5

may claim me whole, the door I rest upon groans open, inwardly this time like an inexplicable trap one could never possibly foresee.

I am cast backward, drawn into the bottomless abyss, a void blacker than the grave, vast and insatiable. It devours with neither mercy nor end, a darkness tearing me from the fragile veil of life. Not even my screams dare trespass upon the thick, unholy silence of this accursed descent.

So, it seems this is death: cold, silent, eternal.

The Candle in the Crypt

Night spilled inky shadows across the crumbling stones of Alderwick Manor. The ancient estate crouched atop the moors like a beast poised to pounce on unsuspecting prey. Its gnarled form blended perfectly with the thick darkness.

For generations, the manor had stood brooding, its windows blind with dust, its doors sagging under the weight of decay and rust. No living soul had dared to inhabit its rooms, not since the night the Morgan family inexplicably vanished.

Now, beneath a waning crescent moon offering only slivers of pale light through the trees, a figure pressed through the iron gate. Selene Morgan, the last of her line, had returned. She who bore the Morgan eyes, turning silver in the moonlight and dark as teary sorrow by day.

Her father's will, penned in a trembling hand and delivered by a solicitor with a hawk-like face, beady eyes, and a smile as cold as stone, had summoned her home to claim what was rightfully hers.

As Selene stood unmoving before the main entrance, she

felt hesitant, as if crossing that line would awaken something best left undisturbed. The wind stirred the wild hedgerows like a distant lament for the family long buried beneath its soil. Even the air felt forlorn with the scent of damp earth, forgotten sorrow, and secrets etched deep into the manor's bones.

She drew her cloak tighter with a shiver, unlocked the door, and stepped inside.

Was coming here a mistake? What could I possibly hope to gain, besides the manor itself?

The manor had its own language. Silence. The place spoke to no one except those with the gift—or curse—to hear its voice.

Every step Selene took on the marble floor echoed like the slow thudding of her heart. Her candlelight flickered across the numerous portraits lining the walls. Fashionably dressed, stern men and women stared down with furtive, painted eyes, as if watching her every move. She hated them all, despised the way their eyes always followed, as though judging her every move.

Moth-eaten drapes sagged on thick wooden rods, hanging down like mournful funeral shrouds. Shadows pooled in the corners, lean and patient. Rope-like spiderwebs clung to the walls as though waiting to ensnare any soul foolish enough to draw near. Selene passed by without a touch, with little thought to spare due to the strange stipulations in her father's will.

It spoke of the crypt beneath the manor—a place she had visited often in her youth—but the insistence on her presence there before she could claim her inheritance seemed more a pointless obstacle than a necessity. After all, what remained here but dirty glass, decay, and the ghosts of old memories?

She knew the stories, the family legends, the old superstitions, all meant to scare children into obedience. But now, standing here, she realized how naive she had been. Something was wrong, no matter if she could put a name to it or not.

Checking her watch to see both hands converged on the midnight hour, she recalled it being the hour her family dreaded most. The veil between worlds was thinnest then, and that was when evil was said to stir, at least according to her mother. Yet Selene, wearied by the ghosts of her past and resolute in her resolve, pressed on. She simply wanted to do her duty and leave, never to lay eyes on Alderwick again.

She located the crypt door by memory, hidden deep in the library where books slumped in their cases like tired old men nursing a hangover. The entrance lay concealed behind a thick tapestry depicting a battle fought long ago. Selene shrank at the sight of it. The grotesque image always unsettled her, even as a child.

"I never realized how awful this thing is. It's sickening. Besides, who would paint a picture of people being slaughtered?" She pointed to the image as though giving a lecture. Her voice rose an octave. "They're being buried alive. How disgusting." She paused, brow furrowing. "Why would anyone hang this atrocity on the wall?"

Moving to the hearth, she traced searching fingers along the baroque molding until they found the hidden latch. With a firm push, it clicked open. A chill surged out, like the breath of a beast long confined, exhaled for the first time in eons. Hesitation gripped her. What family secrets could be so terrible they needed buried with the dead?

The granite staircase was worn smooth. The stone walls were gnawed by time. Smells of rot and dust thickened as she descended. Her candlelight flickered like an irregular heartbeat. The sputtering flame cast monstrous, shifting shapes on the walls. Finally, at the foot of the stairs, Selene stood before a thick wooden door, its weight borne by great iron hinges dark with age. Its surface was etched with tangled glyphs—runes her father once called Morgan Runes. Ancient, binding symbols.

Runes meant to keep something in—or something out. She had no idea which.

With a trembling hand, she slid the iron key, the one given as part of the estate settlement, into the lock. The rusted, ancient mechanism turned with a groan, echoing through the silence like a scream from the past. Selene shuddered as the door creaked open.

Inside, the crypt was vast, its icy air like breath from the long-dead residents. Coffins lined the walls, each one etched with names eroded by centuries of neglect. Yet her gaze was drawn to the center of the crypt, where a single candle burned atop an intricate marble pedestal, its flame impossibly steady in the stifling air.

She moved closer, heart pounding with uncertainty and fear. The candle's wax was black, the flame tinged green— unnatural, casting no shadows. Beneath the pedestal was a plaque: "Here lies the memory of countless sins unspoken."

Her father's whispers returned to her, speaking of tales concerning ancestral curses. And as the story went, from the very beginning of the Morgan line, a single flame was to be kept burning within the crypt. It was said that the candle would remain until the bloodline came to an end. Only then would the flame be snuffed out.

None who had seen it lived to speak of what it illuminated —or what it guarded.

Despair washed over Selene as she recalled the legend.

"I am the last," she whispered, her voice trembling as if speaking the words might shatter her. They did, forcing her to swallow again the bitter note of despair that she could not bear children. She spoke to convince herself more than anything else. "Soon, the flame will gutter, and it shall be over."

From the darkness, whispers rose like dead leaves stirred by the wind or the secretive laughter of the long-buried.

"Morgan," it breathed. The air grew colder.

Selene spun, her eyes searching. The chamber was empty, save for the dead. The candle's flame flared, making the shadows twist, stretching toward her as figures slowly took shape, materializing luminous and insubstantial. She was not alone. Their eyes hollow, their mouths moving in silent agony, they beckoned her closer.

Each step forward proved a struggle. "Why do you linger?" Her voice cracked. "What binds you here? Go rest. Be at peace."

The specters drifted closer, their forms blurring. A chorus of voices, layered and mournful, answered.

"We are bound to the secret. The sin that festers in these stones. Only a Morgan can set us free. You are the one."

Selene's hands shook. She remembered her father's final words: "What's buried must not remain buried. Set the dead free." But she had made no sense of his ramblings then. Still, her desire to know the whole truth was a hunger that had gnawed at her for as long as she could remember.

In that moment, the crypt trembled beneath her, feet as though the walls themselves were alive. She reeled, then lurched to her right. Gripping the candle with one hand as the other clutched frantically at an iron ring set deep into the wall, she found her balance.

Coffins rattled, and from the stone above, a yawning fissure split wide. The flame flared, casting light upon a hidden alcove beneath the pedestal. There, concealed under the smooth, cold marble and the remnants of a once-glorious tomb, lay a small black box sealed with red wax.

Selene knelt. Her breath came in fragments as the box called to her. Hands shaking, she broke the seal. Inside, nestled in rotted velvet, lay a bundle of letters, their edges stained by time.

She opened the topmost envelope, her mind racing with possibilities as she pulled the parchment from its depths. The delicate handwriting belonged to an ancestor. She had seen it before in the Morgan History Book.

Reading on, her face twisted in horror. The world spun as the words revealed a most egregious crime—an entire village reduced to ash. Survivors buried alive or murdered, their bodies cast into a mass grave beneath Alderwick's stones.

From that day, their spirits were bound forever to the Morgan line, a blood price for lands seized by force centuries ago. The candle. The crypt. The curse. Penance for a sin too great to name. Selene felt dizzy with grief.

So that is why I have always hated that painting. It was real! A daily reminder of the atrocity my family performed. For what? Wealth? Land? Greed?

Dark feelings hurriedly swallowed the crypt, complete and suffocating. She froze as the voices rose again. Some were sorrowful, others sharp with rage.

"You see now. You *know*."

More shadows unfurled from the walls, with new ones rising from the floor, coalescing into ghoulish figures. They stood as tattered remnants of lives lost, with painful memories etched on their twisted faces. Some appeared hacked and hewed from sharp weapons. Others looked run through with long pikes or by other horrible means.

"We begged your elders not to do this thing. They would not listen."

One stepped forward—a woman with a torn shawl, clutching something invisible to her chest. A child, perhaps. Her head was flattened on one side as though hit with a tremendous mallet of some type.

"We were promised protection and payment for our lands, but you brought only death. We were not the enemy."

Selene's mouth trembled, unable to form an apology or excuse.

"Your name," a man with a missing arm and horribly damaged face hissed, "should be carved into the stones of this very house. Not as saviors, but as butchers. The Morgans slaughtered us to build a home atop our bones."

The crypt pulsed with anguish, centuries old and still raw.

"We remain against our will. Bound by the spilling of our blood, your utmost betrayal. We come not for vengeance but to be remembered."

Selene bowed her head, ashamed and shivering. "I didn't know. I do—"

"You know now," said one.

"The curse upon your family was never meant to punish you, child. It was meant to awaken you. Set things right," said another. "We cannot move on without you."

The candle flared, though no hand had touched it. The ghosts faded, their edges unraveling like smoke, though their presence lingered—no longer just tormentors, but mourners.

Selene knelt in the stillness, heart heavy with truth. Tears burned as they slid down her cheeks, hot and silent. She leaned forward, touching the flame to the parchment pages. The green fire caught instantly, flaring with a hiss, devouring the confession in a surge of hungry light.

From the shadows, spirits tore free from the walls, groaning with relief as they escaped their once-eternal prison. Her ancestors followed, drifting about with thin, inhuman cries. Drawn into the blaze, they writhed and twisted as the parchment blackened, then curled into ash.

When the last ember faded, the crypt fell deathly silent.

The candle on the pedestal flickered, then slowly died.

Selene stood alone, her own candle seeming weak and insignificant against the encroaching darkness. Her heavy heart suddenly felt unburdened. Above, the manor groaned a centuries-old final breath. The curse had lifted—gone after ages of deceit, lies, and tortured anguish.

When dawn broke, Selene stood at the threshold of Alderwick Manor, the weight of generations lifting from her shoulders like mist on a windy day. The moors fell silent, but in the stillness lay a fragile promise that even in places choked with shadow, ruin, and death, light may yet prevail.

The Connection

Amber closed her car door. Thunder drowned out the sound of her boots shuffling over the asphalt road. Glancing up to watch the moon slide behind thick clouds, she cursed. The storm was moving faster than anticipated. She peered east, then west, her gaze covering both the Millwood Bridge and Grimsley Road.

Both were deserted, save for chirping crickets, croaking toads, and a curious owl hooting from a nearby tree. At this time, she expected nothing less. In fact, she counted on it. How would she explain her situation if spotted? She did not want to consider it. With a quick flick of her wrist, she checked her watch as thunder cracked again. It was closer and louder this time.

" Two a.m.," she grumbled. "I should be sleeping."

She opened the rear passenger door. Reaching inside, she grabbed the bottom edge of the plastic tarp. With a firm tug, the cylindrical object tumbled out, landing on the pavement with a sickening thud. She didn't flinch. Instead, she checked the ropes and weights again. As before, they were tight and secure. Satisfied, she dragged the load toward the edge.

The tarp crinkled and crackled as it twisted in her grip. She grimaced. No matter how many times she did this, she could never get used to that sharp, grating sound. It scraped at her nerves, sending an involuntary shiver down her spine.

To her benefit, Amber was built for this sort of task. She was a fit, thirty-year-old workout fanatic who ate gluten-free food, hated the idea of consuming dead animals, and was a devout vegan. Her firm physique was a source of pride. After all, she had to stay in shape, since disposing of dead bodies took tremendous effort.

Lilith, her partner of sorts, chimed in her ears. *Get rid of this loser before you're spotted.*

Amber dropped the body to clamp both hands over her ears and wait for her unseen accomplice to stop talking. Despite being together since birth, the woman's voice still grated on her nerves even after all these years.

"One would think I would get used to your incessant harping by now! It's been three decades!" She huffed. "I'm doing the best I can. If you're in a such a hurry, you do it."

Very funny. Just get it done, you silly woman. You know I can't help! Should I pull your strings a bit harder, puppet? Part of Lilith's shrill laugh was drowned out by another thunderclap. Drizzle began to fall.

Amber heard enough. Grabbing the tarp and heaving the body upright, she propped it against the railing, hoisted it upward, then flipped its end over to watch the corpse fall the sixty feet. The tightly wrapped body slapped the surface with a loud splash before vanishing into the black depths beneath the swiftly moving water. Another thunder boom rolled overhead as the rain increased.

"Done!" Amber caught her breath, then straightened her clothing. She shivered from the wetness.

See, that wasn't so hard. Now, go find another one.

"The only thing I'm finding is my warm bed before I catch pneumonia," Amber replied, settling into the driver's seat. "Leave me alone for tonight."

Leave me alone. Leave me alone. Lilith mocked in childlike fashion. *I will never leave you alone, we're a great team.*

Amber didn't reply. She sat rigid, thoughts souring as always after a disposal. Lilith's control was unshakable. Wishing her dead was possible but a waste of time. There was no choice other than to endure the woman's torment. They were twins after all, connected in an odd sort of way, and despite it all, Amber carried an unspoken sorrow for her sister.

Frustrated and wet, Amber gripped the steering wheel tighter as memories flooded her mind.

She had always been different from other kids. Thankfully, as she grew up, she had Lilith. The duo grew even closer once Amber could walk and talk. Lilith was always there to soothe her when times were tough or when her twin sister needed a friend. She had been a comforting presence over the years, even more so after Amber realized others did not have her special gift.

Though, she no longer considered her abilities a gift. It became more of a curse than not. But in years past, in a child's mind, her situation was normal, though she often wondered why her playmates did not have their own invisible friends to chat with. If they did, they were afraid to admit it. She felt sorry for the ones who had no one to confide in or tell secrets to.

During her formative years, her parents ignored her having conversations when no one else was present. They merely said she had a vivid imagination. But serious troubles started in kindergarten. Hateful kids did nothing but ridicule, joke, bully, and perform other childish behaviors on the sad little girl. Her plight ramped up within days. Hurtful names became her everyday label: crazy, nuts, insane, stupid, cracked, and more. The one she hated most was freak. At the time, Lilith assured her she was no such thing, but that never fully took away the sting.

Once the school began to raise concerns that the little girl was confused, intellectually challenged, or housed several mental abnormalities, a slew of counselors and psychiatrists became her routine. Many said Amber would outgrow the fantasy of an invisible friend. Some wanted to place her on a plethora of medications or sedate her entirely. Others wished to experiment on her to explore the inner workings of her unique mind, as they called it. And they would have had she not quickly learned to keep her mouth shut about Lilith, especially the part about the two of them having long conversations—like best friends are supposed to do. She also learned that, as is the way with most humans, anything or anyone different is shunned and hated. She proved no different.

Even now, decades later, the cruelties of childhood still haunted her. Amber never could recall how or why Lilith entered her head. She just knew they had always been linked by some supernatural bond, one Lilith took full advantage of at times, and grew more so with each passing year alongside her hard and hateful demeanor.

Snapping back to the present, with a turn of the key, she let the engine roar to life. "I'm just special. Not a freak," Amber announced with an edgy voice as she flicked on her high beams and pressed the gas pedal.

Some long minutes later, she turned left into the Lierzton Village subdivision, took another quick left onto Sawgrass Drive, then headed for Stratford Place, three blocks away. Her home lay nestled in a quiet cul-de-sac and served her well. It was perfect, isolated within an upscale neighborhood, but not entirely closed off from humanity.

Inside, she broke open a cardboard box, slit the plastic wrap, then jammed her frozen meal into the microwave. She poured herself a tall glass of ice water, then waited for the beep. Meanwhile, her cat, Gracie, leapt onto the table to rub her forehead and nose against Amber's cheek, purring all the while.

"I missed you, too," cooed Amber, stroking the kitty's back and tail softly.

After having a meal, taking a hot shower, and feeding Gracie, Amber headed for bed. Giving a glance over her shoulder, she pursed her lips, then pushed her tongue against her teeth to make a clicking sound.

"Come on, Miss Cutie." The cat leapt down gracefully and followed, her soft paws tapping a rhythmic sound. Soon, the pair snuggled into bed and fell fast asleep.

————

Why are you still in bed? Get up. We have work to do.

"Shut up, will you! It's Saturday and I want to sleep in." Amber stretched and rubbed the sleep from her eyes, then glanced at the clock. Nine a.m. "Later than I normally sleep in," she noted with a frown.

Let's go shopping. There are always people around. We will find another—

"I hate shopping," Amber retorted while petting Gracie, who remained fast asleep by her side. "Too many damned people. And I did what you asked last night so leave me alone."

Come on! You're getting boring in your old age.

"Excellent! Finally!" Amber shouted, sitting bolt upright to throw her arms in the air. Gracie yawned and looked bothered. "Then why don't you disappear forever, and I can be as freakin' boring as I want. How nice would that be! Just me, my cat, and my books." She pointed to the door. "You . . . gone!"

The shrill, cackling laughter retuned. *Funny little girl, we are together forever. You will never be rid of me. I'm your sister and best friend. Hell, I am your only friend.*

That bit struck a chord in Amber's heart. Her pride was stinging over the truth. "How can I have any friends when you make me act crazy when I'm with them? Shit, I haven't been laid in six months. And you made me kill him!"

No matter. He was a married man cheating on his wife. He deserved to die. You did it yourself. I had nothing to do with it. There was a silent pause as if that news needed to sink in. *Besides, he wasn't right for you. He had a tiny little—*

"Stop! I will not discuss this." Amber eased out of bed, slid into her spandex running outfit, placed her new runners on, and headed for the door. Stuffing AirPods in her ears, she snatched up her phone, found the Pandora app, then turned on the Vivaldi's *The Four Seasons* violin concertos. She loved classical music. It relaxed her and drowned Lilith out.

After feeding Gracie again, she gave her cat a kiss between the ears. Amber closed the door and took to the street.

As the pavement passed under her feet in steady fashion, she came across a little girl sitting on the curb crying. No more than six or seven, her legs were drawn up close, her chin rested on both knees, and her small arms encircled them to hold her steady. Her back heaved up and down with each sob.

Amber lowered next to the child. Taking her phone out, she paused the music. "My name is Amber. What's the matter, hun?"

The little girl sucked in short breaths and wiped her eyes on her sleeve. "Mom and Dad are fighting. They always do. Dad hit Mom again this morning. I hate him and want him to disappear."

I like this kid! She has the right idea. Go kill the pig. It's what we do.

Amber mentally pushed Lilith away, but it was a struggle. "What's your name, sweetheart?"

More sniffing and short, gasping breaths. "Luna."

"My, that's a beautiful name." Amber rubbed her back gently, then went on. "Luna, do you have a friend's house you can go to?"

Luna nodded and pointed to a solid brick house four doors away. "Jamie lives there. It's where I always go when things get bad."

Amber helped the girl stand, then pointed across the street. "Why don't you head over there and someone will come get you later? I'll watch to make sure you get there. Everything will be fine. I'll see to it."

Finally! Kill him now! Cut off both his miserable hands as penalty for hitting his wife. Leave out the cops and handle it yourself.

Amber gritted her teeth in response. She desperately wanted to scream at Lilith. Instead, she patted Luna's back. "Go on. I will handle this. Mom and Dad will never fight again."

Luna frowned and kicked a rock. "That's impossible. But thank you anyway."

"Go on, now. Everything will be fine." Amber shooed her away, waving as the little girl looked over her shoulder while ambling down the street. When she disappeared into her friend's home, Amber let her arm drop.

"Maybe you're right this time, Lilith. I can't stand by while this clown smacks his wife around."

Egged on by her sister's victorious cry, Amber stormed down the sidewalk toward the house. But before she could step foot on the lawn, the front door swung open. A tirade of shouting flowed out like a wave of hateful energy spilling into the tranquil morning, rising from the throat of a rather handsome, muscular man. Stomping outside, he slammed the door, then walked toward the community park.

"Going to cool off, I bet." Amber formulated a quick plan. Jogging past, she caught the man's eye and winked, then waved. He took the hint, waved back, then picked up his pace, half walking, half jogging. But he was no match for Amber's stride. Within seconds, she left him far behind.

In the park, she awaited his arrival, hoping he would be stupid enough to show himself. He definitely seemed the arrogant kind who believed he was a gift to women. Clearly, he would fool around on his wife . . . especially after a fight.

Minutes passed before he appeared. But as he looked around, searching with a foul eagerness, second thoughts began to fill Amber's head. What was she doing? She couldn't—

You know what to do. This weak-minded moron deserves to die for what he has done.

"Agreed," Amber replied, surprising herself with the ease of which she just condemned another man to death. "But I wish it wasn't so soon. We just finished one last night. I can't keep this up forever. I'll be caught if I do."

Wicked is wicked, honey. There is no end to the hate and anger in the world. Vermin like this must be dealt with. Even Luna said this happened a lot. Her sister's voice faded for several long moments. *Do you want the poor girl to watch her mommy get beat again? Maybe someday the pig will turn his anger on the little girl. Is that what you want?*

"Oh, that was a low blow," Amber muttered. She considered the words, then gave a slow nod as a long sigh escaped from her lips. "You're right. Something needs to be done."

Lilith's voice sounded excited. *And you are just the woman to do it. Look, here comes the idiot now.*

Luna's father had spotted her. His gait quickened, heading straight for the bench Amber patiently waited on. He stopped before her as if posing for a magazine cover. Meeting her eyes, he flashed a toothy grin while casually reaching to scratch his crotch, so her eyes were drawn there from reflex. He seemed to get a thrill from her unintentional glance. Lowering onto the wooden bench, he introduced himself as Ryan and began to talk.

Amber did not care what he called himself. She only felt her disdain at being near a wife beater. His mere appearance and behavior disgusted her. To hurry things along, she slid close to place her warm hand on his inner thigh. Tracing small, teasing circles, she easily wrangled him into a date, one he eagerly accepted.

"Ten o'clock tonight. Meet me by Lincoln's statue in Wilson's Park. The gates close before that, but if you jump the fence down by Porter Street, we can be alone." She winked and edged her hand up closer to his manhood, making him squirm with feverish anticipation.

That's my girl! So proud of you. Soon, he won't be hitting anyone else.

To seal the deal, Amber leaned in to brush her full lips against his cheek while whispering suggestively in his ear. Not waiting for what would surely be a gross, enthusiastic response, she sprang up and jogged on. Running harder, she fumed at her repulsive behavior, unable to shake the man's leering behavior from her mind. It clung to her, wriggling like a foreign entity under her skin.

The moment she arrived home, she showered to rid herself of his vile feeling. Afterward, she prepared her murder kit. Rope, gloves, shovel, zip ties, flashlight, and other items she was unsure if she would need or not. Better too much than too little, she thought to Lilith's appreciative chuckle. She changed into old clothing from a secondhand store, placed her gear in the back of her Subaru, then went inside to read.

Time passed excruciatingly slowly. Yet, all the same, it finally arrived. Before departing, she spent several minutes petting Gracie. "The kitty door is open if you want to go play. Stay behind the fence and do not invite strange animals in the house. Oh, I will be home late." She scratched the cat's chin, gave her a hug, then kissed her head before placing her on the floor. Convinced the fluffy gray cat understood her every word, she added, "Don't wait up." Gracie rubbed against her leg and meowed.

———

Excluding the long cement walkways lit by evenly spaced lampposts, the park's only illumination came by means of a sliver of moonlight peering down from the cloudless sky. Stepping from the trail meant entering the darkness at your own risk.

"You never can tell what wicked things hide themselves away in deep shadows," Amber said softly. She chuckled at her own joke.

Well said. We are going to be the wicked things tonight. Lilith laughed her cackling sound.

The towering trees swayed in the light breeze. Outside the reach of the man-made glow, the grass looked as though it were a dark, undulating ocean moving in time with the barked behemoths acting as guardians. She wondered if the trees and grass spoke to one another.

Amber checked her watch, then backed deeper into the darkness. She kept the towering stone image of President Lincoln to her side. Ten minutes to go. She wondered if Ryan would back out. Maybe he was too busy smacking his wife around again to show up. Her ears grew warm at the thought. Her fingers pressed into her palms forming fists of rage.

That's right, get angry! Use that hate to do what needs done!

"Shush. I hear something." Amber tilted her head in the direction of the trail.

Faint whistling came forward as Ryan emerged from the thin veil of shadows. He wore jeans and a t-shirt. New, expensive Nike's graced his feet and his long brown ponytail swayed as he walked happily along. There was a growing grin on his face.

This smug shit thinks he's getting lucky tonight. We'll show him.

"Yes, we will." Amber stepped into the light. "Pssst, Ryan," she said softly before fading back into the thickening night.

He approached eagerly, moving across the lawn with steady steps. After running both hands through his hair and licking his lips, he came to a halt and eyed her muscular form in the pale moonlight.

Amber tried to look pleased even as his gaze made her feel dirty again. When he reached for her, she slipped back further, almost holding up a hand. "You didn't tell anyone about our meeting, did you?" she whispered.

Ryan displayed a distasteful look. "For shit's sake, I'm not stupid. Of course not."

"Oh baby, I knew you were a genius." Amber stepped closer to run her hand over his tight stomach. Her fingers trailed down between his legs to massage his pride and joy. He tilted his head back to moan.

Now, both Lilith and Amber's own thoughts voiced, for once in total harmony.

Ryan never noticed the singular, soft click. Suddenly, his world turned hazy as the noise grew loud, steady, and painful. His eyes rolled back. His limbs shook as he stood horribly trapped in the throes of pain. Spittle ran down his chin before he collapsed to the ground with a thump.

Amber laughed at his pitiful form, then kicked his leg to be sure he was quite helpless. She switched off her stun gun and stowed it in her small pack, the one she had hidden in the bushes earlier.

Lilith mirrored her laughter. *Idiot! Now you'll get what's coming to you. Go on, beat his head in with the shovel.*

"No, I will not." Amber zip-tied his hands behind his back. She secured his feet next. One dirty sock went in his mouth, and a wide piece of duct tape held it firmly in place.

Slowly regaining awareness, Ryan panicked, kicking and thrashing about as he gained control of his faculties.

"Stop it, you asshole." Amber kicked him hard in the ribs, then rapidly freed her stun gun and pressed it to his stomach to give another long jolt. He lapsed into unconsciousness, but not before soiling himself.

See, men can be obedient if you treat them right. Lilith laughed. *Kill him and let's be done.*

"Patience," Amber replied, rubbing her chin. "Before he dies, he's going to know why I'm doing this. He's going to know what hell he's put his wife and daughter through. And he's going to beg me not to kill him." She laughed, not unlike the sound Lilith made. "But I won't listen to his bullshit. In fact, I changed my mind. I won't even let him talk."

Do it now!

Amber waved a dismissive hand and carried on. She dragged Ryan through the level woods, purposely running his head over every rock she could see. It took her some time before she found the perfect spot: the one he would spend eternity in.

After a search of his pockets for weapons, she only found a handful of condoms. "Moron," she said before dragging him another five feet and securing him to a thick oak tree. Then she hurriedly dashed back to retrieve her remaining gear.

Upon returning, she used the shovel to remove the top grass layer with ease. She turned over the topsoil, forming it into sod rolls which she set aside before digging a grave directly at his feet. Again, Ryan showed signs of slowly waking from his stupor, panicking and struggling against his bonds.

Look at him! Not so tough now, is he? Pluck his eyes out and feed them to him! Cut that thing off from between his legs. Feed him that, too!

"Will you stop," Amber insisted. "I'm going to kill him, not dismember him. Imagine the mess I'd make."

Those words sent Ryan into a fit. But struggle as he might, his weakened state was no match for the strong ties and thick ropes. Tears streamed from his eyes as his head lolled from one side to the other. He mumbled unintelligible sounds through his gag.

Amber neither listened nor cared. Finally, the hole was done. Her eyes met his. Power coursed through her veins. Ultimate control was what she had. She inched closer, straddling his lap with her strong thighs. Her lips dropped to his ear, and he went still.

"It's not so much fun being abused, is it, you piece of shit?" she whispered. "Now you understand the helpless feeling your wife has when you beat her. And you make your precious daughter watch it all, you asswipe." She lashed out a hard right hand to connect with his jaw. His head snapped back, impacting the tree with force. Dazed, he shook his head before giving another pointless struggle. Tears ran down his cheeks as his eyes pleaded silently for mercy.

He disgusts me. End this! There is more justice to be handed out in the world. Let's move on.

"When I'm ready," Amber snapped as she edged forward to grind her hips onto his groin.

His wild eyes searched the darkened woods for the partner his assailant spoke to, not realizing she was quite alone. Mostly, anyway. Terrified wriggling and squirming redoubled as muffled noises emanated from under his nose.

Amber leaned in to kiss the tape covering his mouth. With a practiced hand, she moved to caress his cheek.

"This is for your wife and daughter, shithead." She slid the ice pick into his ear canal and pushed the point into his brain until the handle stopped. Ryan's body jerked. His eyes stared upward endlessly as she pulled it free.

His head fell forward as blood drained from his ear. Amber rose to stare, tilting her head as if confused by what she had done.

No time to waste. Let the worms have him. Bury him.

"I'm getting to it. Relax." Amber loosened the ropes and with a heave, jerked the corpse forward to watch it fall prone into the deep hole. "Perfect. No one will ever see your face again." Tugging the shovel free of the dirt pile, she backfilled her handiwork.

By 2 a.m., Amber had nearly finished. She rolled the sod layers into place and patted them with the shovel. With a final smile at her work, she spit on the grass.

"I hope the gods punish you for eternity."

Fine work, dear! Fine work, indeed!

Within an hour, she was home. She fed the cat, cleaned and stowed her tools, ate a healthy supper, and took a hot shower. Exhausted, she and Gracie curled up in bed to sleep.

Soon, the pair fell fast asleep. Though Amber tossed and turned, unable to escape the nightmare of the night her life had forever changed. The night that ripped her folks away. She awoke more than once, gasping for breath, and each time, she remembered the solace that Lilith, at least, had been spared from the auto accident.

She jerked the comforter to her chin and squeezed both eyes shut, waiting for a semblance of sleep to take her away.

Miles away in the Restful Woods community, a nurse set a tray on a round, white table, then pulled a chair next to a young woman to wipe the drool from her lips. Her vegetative patient barely acknowledged her presence.

The kind nurse scooped the soft mush from the plate and held it out. "Here we go," she said in an encouraging tone, sliding the spoonful of green slop past the woman's lips.

The nurse demonstrated a chewing motion as if teaching a child. "Isn't this wonderful food, Lilith? It keeps you strong and healthy. Eat up. Only the best for our longest resident."

Another spoonful entered her mouth as Lilith stared mindlessly out the window, her jaw working from muscle memory alone.

Inheritance

T he box arrived on a Tuesday afternoon, during a lull
in the rain. Ben Ashwood watched the delivery
driver through his doorbell cam, puzzling over the
mystery package's arrival.

Nonetheless, the curious box remained on his doorstep
until he arrived home. He stared at it. *At least the correct
address is on it.* Wrapped in rough burlap, sealed with purple
wax, and tied with fraying twine, the small square—the size of
an old lunchbox he had carried as a kid—sat in silent wait. No
postage, no sender information, just a tag yellowed with age
tucked into the knot like an afterthought.

'For Benjamin Ashwood. A gift, long overdue.'

Plain and simple. I like that. Handling it with care, he
brought it inside, set it on the kitchen table, and stared again for
a long while, like it might blink or move. *I've watched too many
damned horror movies. Just open the stupid thing. It's not like
Chucky is inside . . . or is he?*

When curiosity rose to a point of intolerance, Ben moved to

unwrap his surprise. He could tell right away that the box itself was old. This was not some mass-produced piece of junk. There were no barcodes or branding. Just solid, heavy wood, nearly black, carved with an elaborate pattern of symbols and vines that looked Celtic in design. In the center of the lid was a crest he did not recognize: a tree split down the middle, mirrored roots and branches tangled together like veins.

Even as his suspense built upon itself, he hesitated, then breathed deeply and lifted the lid.

Inside was a small brass key and a piece of parchment folded three times over. The silk lining's color had faded to a bruised purple. The paper crinkled in his hand as he read the exquisite, slanted handwriting that bore similarities to a style from an ancient, long-forgotten manuscript.

Ashwood blood runs deep. Turn the key and discover who you truly are.

Ben pondered those words for a long while, not knowing what he had been expecting. A prank? Some kind of performance art? Regardless, the weight of the gift, the way the key felt cold even in his warm hand, made him uneasy.

That night, after hours of internal debate while smoking a fat joint, he sat alone, holding the box in his lap. The city outside was quiet. The earlier storm had passed, and everything smelled fresh and clean.

He slid the key into the small slot, trembling as he turned it. There was a sharp, metallic click, like the snapping of a small, brittle bone. For a heartbeat, everything calmed. Then, with a deafening crack, the overhead light shattered in a burst of sparks, sending a shower of hot glass scattering across the floor.

The room went black.

A low, unnatural hum vibrated through the floor, deep and unsettling, making the hairs on his neck stand on end. The walls pulsed with it, breathing in time with the horrible sound. A shiver of cold rolled around the room, stealing his warmth. Mist poured from the box's seams—dense, swirling, and creeping outward.

Thick and ghostly, the fog spun and twisted with a strange, almost sentient purpose.

Ben tried to move, to back away, but he was held firm by an unseen force. He could only push himself deeper into the couch cushions. His body was paralyzed by something far beyond fear. With a groan that rattled his entire apartment, the ground shifted unsteadily beneath his feet.

Disoriented and free now, he tossed the box aside and fumbled for a light switch. His foot caught a piece of furniture, sending him falling into the darkness. He remembered no more.

———

Waking face-down in mud, Ben gasped for breath like someone pulled from underwater.

The scent hit him first—wet earth, pine needles, distant smoke. Pushing himself to a sitting position, he rubbed his head. Gone were the apartment walls, the carpet underfoot, the ceiling overhead. He was in a clearing surrounded by dense, towering trees that blotted out the sky. It was cold. Damp. He touched the mud, and his fingers came away dark and sticky. Real, not some haunting dream.

At his feet, the box sat undisturbed on a patch of moss, its silken interior dry despite the mist curling around him. Ben stared at it, then at his hands, then at the narrow dirt path snaking into the woods.

Gaining his footing, he followed it, the box clutched tight in his arms like a lifeline.

Obsession took root quickly. The possibilities ignited in his mind, each one sparking a new thread of wonder, a new path to chase. He could not stop imagining how far it might go, what secrets it might still hold, or what secrets he could learn. The power of space and time were his.

———

The box did not simply transport him through space. It dragged him through time. At first, the trips were sporadic. He would simply touch the key and vanish, only to awaken in some past century, sometimes still in the woods, sometimes amid cobbled streets or barren farmlands or places that no longer existed in the modern world.

Over time, he learned that intention mattered. If he focused—on a name, a year, a place—the box responded. Not entirely a precise procedure, but close enough.

Eventually, curiosity turned inward as he began researching his family. Ashwood, while not a rare name, was not common either. He dug through online archives, visited local historical societies, and even bribed an archivist in Philadelphia to access restricted genealogies.

The deeper he searched, the more the name *Isaiah Ashwood* surfaced. There were fragments of sermons, references in journals, and trial records that had been redacted or destroyed. Isaiah had been a preacher in the early 1800s, a veteran of the War of 1812, and a self-proclaimed demon-hunter in a Puritan village named Lark Hollow.

More disturbingly, Isaiah had been accused of causing a string of disappearances—young women mostly—and suspected of executing them under the guise of exorcisms or purifications. Officially, he died of Fever and was buried in

33

sanctified ground. But the side notes, the whispers in letters and diaries, told a different story.

Isaiah Ashwood did not die peacefully. He simply vanished.

With the force of a runaway train, it came to him. Ben knew what he had to do.

He opened the box, fixed the year *1811* in his mind, then whispered the name *Isaiah Ashwood*, all while picturing the forest settlement of Lark Hollow—a place he knew only from the sketches he had uncovered in his research.

Taking a calming breath, he turned the key.

———

He landed in a world colder and harsher than the one he had left and far different than what he had expected. Lark Hollow sat like a festering wound in the woods—gray houses, crooked fences, rutted roads, and villagers who stared back with suspicion and decades of trauma in their eyes.

For days, Ben kept to the shadows, observing from the edges of the village, careful not to draw attention. Eventually, under cover of darkness, he stole a plain outfit from a backyard clothesline— worn but clean, the sort of thing no one would miss. With it, he blended in just enough. Food, he stole, too. *What choice do I have?*

When Sunday morning finally came, he made his way toward the church. If Isaiah was what the records suggested, that would be the place to start.

Moving through the narrow, muddy streets, he noticed again how the villagers avoided his gaze. No one greeted him, yet no one challenged him either. He was a stranger, clearly— but for now, he did not stand out.

And then he saw him.

There was no mistaking the man. Isaiah Ashwood stood on the steps of the church, shaking hands, nodding solemnly as townsfolk filed inside. His long robes hung stiffly from his shoulders, black against the graying sky. He smiled as he welcomed them—pleasant on the surface, almost warm.

Isaiah's eyes never shone bright like the rest of his face. Still, he was a handsome man—striking, even. His jaw was square, his cheekbones sharp, his nose narrow and slightly upturned, giving him a refined, almost noble look. He appeared surprisingly youthful for a man of his reputation.

Ben guessed he was no more than thirty-five, which aligned with his research. But there was an edge to him, something too precise in the way he carried himself. His posture looked rigid, almost confrontational. His gestures were measured, like every movement had been rehearsed.

Beneath it all, there was a creepy hollowness behind his eyes, like a lantern with no flame.

From a safe distance, Isaiah looked like a man revered. Yet, this was not simply charisma, it was control. Power and anger disguised as piety, barely suppressed, but steadied by years of practice. The way he held their attention, the quiet fear behind their lowered eyes, all made sense now.

Up close, Ben suspected he was feared. This was not just a man corrupted by power; his soul was evil.

"Of course," he muttered. "Madness wrapped in scripture. Or maybe not wrapped at all."

The resemblance between the two men was uncanny. The face Ben had only seen in yellowed portraits stared back at him in the flesh—same bone structure, same slanted brow, same quiet, deliberate gait. It was more than resemblance. It was reflection. And it terrified him.

He watched Isaiah move through the growing crowd with

practiced ease. A nagging question lodged itself in Ben's mind like a festering splinter.

If blood carries history, what else might it carry? Madness, perhaps, curled like a snake in my DNA, lingering within my soul.

Ben thought of himself as a good, decent man. Kind, even. He had never hurt anyone. Not really. But could a person ever truly judge their own sanity? Isn't that what madness does—convinces you that you are whole while something inside you rots and turns to vile wickedness? And if not yourself, then who could judge you?

Certainly not some absent god, hiding behind unanswered prayers. No—Ben had come to believe something much more sinister: that under the right pressure, with the right push, a killer lay dormant in every one of us. The question was not whether the bloodline was cursed. The question was how close he already stood to the edge of becoming Isaiah.

As the preacher shuffled his flock inside, Ben followed, taking a distant seat in the pews far from the pulpit. From there, he watched Isaiah preach damnation and fury from his haven within the church walls.

The sanctuary, once a place of warmth and mercy, now trembled with a different kind of fire. Shadows danced along the stained-glass windows, bleeding through with the blood-colored light of the setting sun. The pulpit groaned beneath Isaiah's weight as he slammed a fist against it, his voice rising with conviction.

"The world is sick!" he roared, spittle flying from cracked lips. "And you—all of you—have swallowed its poison like wine!"

The congregation sat rigid, eyes wide, breath held. Some nodded, entranced. Others flinched with each accusation.

"The sinners walk proud and free in daylight now! They

entice you with sly words while spitting in the face of God, then dare ask for mercy!" His voice rustled, but he pressed on. "Mark my words, judgment is coming, and it will not come with whispers, but fire!"

Ben sat near the back, half-concealed by a warped pillar as Isaiah's words peeled flesh from spirit. The man was no longer a shepherd of faith. He was a prophet of wrath. His once-kind face twisted with something venomous, ancient, and hungry.

"There is no forgiveness without blood." Isaiah's eyes scanned the pews like a hawk circling carrion. "You want peace? Then repent with your whole being—or burn alongside the godless!" He raised a hand, trembling with fervor. "The Lord does not forget. Neither does my God forgive those who mock Him. And neither do I."

A cold hush fell. Not holy silence—something else. Something like fear.

When the hateful sermon finally ended, there was no gentle benediction. No promise of grace. Just Isaiah, standing like a monument to fury, watching his flock with eyes like judgment itself.

Ben stumbled outside, gasping for air. He left feeling weak, lost, and filled with despair. The cool wind did nothing to shake the weight from his chest. Isaiah's words echoed in his mind like a curse etched in stone. He no longer knew if he was saved—or marked.

Slinking back into the woods, Ben waited to follow Isaiah home. It was the cleanest, largest house in the village. *Now I know where you are!*

Then, one evening after slipping from the barn he had been secretly sleeping in, Ben watched the home, knowing Isaiah had to leave sometime.

Patience proved his ally. Within a few hours, Isaiah strode into the night to slip inside a decaying barn on the far outskirts of the village. Ben followed in secret, careful of his every step. Sneaking closer, he peered into a crack in the wall. There, he saw what Isaiah truly was.

A girl, no more than thirteen, was cruelly tied to a wooden post. Her face was bruised, her mouth gagged. Isaiah stood before her, chanting in Latin, holding a knife curved like a crescent moon. His voice was steady, devoid of empathy. As his chanting continued, he cut her here and there, paying no mind to her stifled screams of agony.

Ben could not stand by and watch. He burst through the door without a solid plan.

Isaiah turned, not startled—but expectant. As if expecting his arrival.

"Blood recognizes blood," he murmured. "Thou are part of me, are you not? Family. Welcome, bearer of my blood, my son."

Ben froze. "I am not your son." His reply was all he could manage.

Isaiah stepped closer, his eyes alive with madness. "Thy face hath appeared in my dreams. Lo! First, I deemed you the Devil. But that role belongs to another. Verily, thou dost portray a living portrait of myself, mine own shadow." With a flick of the blade, he cut the girl again for spite, laughing as the steel drew blood. "Now, thou standest before me in vain if ye mean to cease my purification of this foul creature?" He eyed the girl with a wicked glance. "A demon dwells within and must be cleansed."

He raised the knife again. Ben lunged forward, his fist connecting with a surprised Isaiah, who dropped to one knee from the impact.

The preacher rose with a powerful swing that Ben ducked.

The two tangled in mortal combat, tumbling into the straw

where they fought on, driven by hate and anger. Isaiah was faster, stronger, fueled by something ancient and twisted.

Ben cried out as the steel blade passed over his arm, then his chest. With a quick move, his leg lashed outward, his shin burying itself in Isaiah's groin, collapsing his form to the ground in an agonized, moaning pile of flesh.

The knife clattered to the ground. Ben swiftly kicked it aside before seizing a nearby axe. He raised it to shoulder height, swinging in a wide arc to sever the ropes binding the prisoner. Without hesitation, he grabbed the half-naked girl and, together, they fled into the woods, leaving Isaiah writhing in pain and spewing broken verbal hatred after them.

Rushing her back to the village, Ben left her at the local constabulary home, then vanished into the forest.

Uncovering his belongings from their hiding spot, he took the box and returned to the present. But as before, it did not end there.

———

In the days that followed, something inside him began to rot. The fire Isaiah had lit in the church did not die with the sermon—it smoldered in Ben's chest, scorching everything it touched. He tried to convince himself nothing had changed, but he knew better. His hands trembled at odd moments. Shadows lingered too long in corners. He spoke less, even to himself.

And his dreams grew to be awful. Each night brought some new horror. He woke breathless, drenched in sweat, the sheets twisted tight in his fists as though he'd been grappling with an unseen enemy.

But it was always the same face in the dark—Isaiah's— looming, furious, eternal. Preaching not at a pulpit, but at the edge of Ben's bed. Voice like thunder. Eyes filled with judgment. Fingers pointing at him.

"Blood remembers."

That phrase echoed, worm-like, burrowing into the quiet spaces of his waking mind.

Awful thoughts took root there, slow and deliberate, like mold spreading through the walls of an old house. Was this madness part of him now? Or had it always been? Was it blood-deep? A sickness etched into his lineage. A curse passed from marrow to marrow like a sickening, twisted heirloom.

He thought of his grandfather's silence. His mother's eyes—so often vacant, so often red-rimmed. The rage that sometimes welled in him without cause, without warning. He'd always blamed the world for that heat. But now he wondered. Could it be inherited? A taint that lived in the bones, waiting? A sleeping thing, stirring only when called by anger or fear?

One night, hours past midnight, Ben sat alone on the floor. The only light came from a flickering bulb overhead, swinging slightly with the summer draft. His gaze locked on the box—the one he'd sworn he wouldn't open again—and the small iron key beside it.

His hands were steady. Perfectly, unnaturally steady.

"Enough." He whispered the word aloud. Not as a prayer. Not a resolution. But a verdict.

He would go back. One last time. Not to find answers, nor for peace. This time, he would end it.

Whatever *it* truly was.

———

It was still 1811.

Lark Hollow burned.

Villagers screamed in the distance. The church was

engulfed in towering orange flames, its steeple black against the smoke-choked sky. Isaiah stood at the center of it all, robes tattered, his mouth frothing with some violent sermon.

Ben knew what to do.

He sprinted through the fire and slammed into Isaiah. The two fell into the dirt, grappling. Isaiah laughed—mad, triumphant—as the knife flashed between them. Ben knocked the blade away, but before he could grab it, his adversary pounced on him, locking his arms to his sides.

"Lo! Thou comest again, fool! Dost thou believe that slaying me shall deliver thee? Nay, heathen! I deem thee already as I am. Our lives run the same course, knave. So it hath been since thou didst draw thy first breath of life."

Ben—refusing to accept madness was in his makeup—screamed with fury as he threw Isaiah aside and lunged for the blade. Grabbing it, he aimed the sharpened point toward Isaiah's throat and pounced. But the preacher twisted away.

Once more, they engaged in deadly struggle until—at long last, with a quick dip of Ben's shoulder and a powerful strike—Isaiah's body went limp, moving no more.

Ben staggered to his feet, blood on his hands as the world spun around him. Looking down, he grimaced at the intricate handle protruding from Isaiah's chest. The preacher lay dying in a pool of his own blood by his own torturous blade.

"Die knowing you have failed, spawn of Satan!" Ben spat on the ground.

Turning away, he moved into the night to retrieve his box and key.

Ben's apartment looked the same, but his books were unfamiliar. Family photos on the wall were gone. The mail was addressed to him, but no sender seemed familiar. There were no traces of his ancestry online. The Ashwood line had vanished from every database. And yet—he was still here. Alive.

And in the shadows of his bedroom, yet unseen, lay Isaiah's knife, its blade gleaming faintly upon the table.

Patiently waiting to begin again.

The Book of Echoes

I t was late afternoon when the storm rolled in. Thick, dark clouds blotted out the sun. Gusting winds howled through the trees as though warning of something unspeakable yet to come. In the heart of the small village of Filmore, nestled between the ancient, towering elm trees and the mist-covered hills, stood the old Miller farmhouse where the respectable family had lived for generations.

Inside, an orange fire crackled within the hearth, casting flickering shadows on the stone walls. Agatha and her younger brother, Danny, sat cross-legged on the floor, their faces illuminated by the warmth of the flames. Their grandparents, Martha and Tom Miller, sat in their usual fireside chairs, their expressions a mix of warmth and contentedness.

Agatha could not recall a time when she had not loved the old house. It felt alive—the creaky floors, the smell of leather-bound books lining the shelves, and the deep, comforting silence that clung to the walls. It made the outside world seem surreal.

But today, there was a feeling creeping into Agatha's heart.

Everything felt oppressive somehow, like the air itself was thick with riddles or mysteries waiting to be revealed.

Her grandmother, Martha—an avid reader for decades—was the one the young girl worried about. Agatha watched her with quiet concern. The old woman's gaze was distant as she meandered toward the shelf, her fingers trailing along the worn spines until they paused on an ancient book bound in cracked black leather. The title, embossed in faded gold, read simply: *The Book of Echoes*. She carefully pulled the book from the shelf to place it on the table.

The room grew silent for a long moment. Even the crackling fire seemed to hold its breath.

"Grandma, what's that?" Danny asked, his voice filled with curiosity and a hint of apprehension. Only eight, he was still too young to understand the full weight of many things done in their home, and Agatha thought this would be one of those times.

Martha grinned thinly while feeling the book's edges with a reverence. Her voice came low and steady. "A book of power. But also, a book of great cost. Grandpa and I are fading, as is part of life. So now is the time to pass this to you two. It's a gift from our ancestors."

"What do you mean? A gift?" asked Agatha.

Grandma nodded slowly, her eyes darkening. "This book can do many things. It can summon things—dark things—and it can also restore life. But every action has a price, one that shall always be higher than you believe. You must use it wisely, my dears."

Danny leaned forward, his eyes going wide. "Has anyone ever used it before? And can it bring people back? Like . . . like . . . ya' know . . . Mom and Dad?"

Agatha stiffened. Their parents had died in a car accident within a year of her brother's birth, and the pain of their loss never truly went away, despite her grandparents saying time would make everything easier. In many ways, they were right, but it still hurt beyond comprehension.

Luckily, they had Martha and Tom to raise them. They loved them like their own. But the ache of missing parents remained razor sharp.

Martha's gaze softened. "Yes, Danny. It has been used, but the results turned out quite poorly. And, yes, it can bring people back. But you must understand that nothing in this world comes without a cost. To restore life, you must give life in return."

Danny frowned. "What do you mean?"

Tom spoke up from his chair, his voice rough with age. "The book needs balance to act. For every life you restore, something else must be taken or given in its place. Such is the price of power."

Agatha tilted her head in confusion. "You're saying if we bring someone back, someone else has to die?"

Her grandmother nodded solemnly. "That is the cost. And the price is never something you can control. It will always take more than you expect. In the long run, you may be worse off than when you started out."

The concept of bringing back their parents was tempting to Agatha, yet so painful its weight smothered her. Still, somewhere inside, she knew her grandparents were right—no magic came without a price. But she could not look away from the strange book. The spark of hope was lit. With it came questions she could not ignore. *Can it be done? Can they really return?*

Martha gently closed the book. "You must choose wisely, for once you open it, there is no turning back."

The fire writhed and danced as the storm intensified, its winds rattling the windows. Tom rose to put more wood on the fire before retaking his seat.

45

Agatha eyed the book again. She could not help herself. She was itching to open it, to see what secrets lay within its pages. But she knew better. She had to resist. For if she did not, everything could be lost.

As the night wore on, the children went to bed, but the idea of the book and its promises continued to plague Agatha. Could it really bring their parents back? Would she really make such a sacrifice? The cost seemed horrendous. Besides, she had nothing to offer—no life to give away. Even the thought felt repulsive. She was old enough to know trading lives was immoral. And whose would she trade? Grandma? Grandpa? Her brother?

She lay awake for hours, tossing and turning as the decision haunted her every thought. And then, in the dead of night, she heard a soft, haunting whisper.

Open it.

Sitting bolt upright, she glanced around the room. Empty—only the darkness pressing in from every corner.

Open the book, Agatha. You know you want to.

It was her mother's voice. She was sure of it. Her sweet sound was something she would never forget.

Trembling, she slunk from her bed and crept downstairs, her stocking feet barely making a sound on the wooden floor. The fire was long extinguished, and the house was eerily still. The book sat on the table where her grandma had left it, its dark cover gleaming faintly in the flickering candlelight.

Agatha reached for it. She could not resist. The longing, the ache to see her parents again, to hold them just once more, was too powerful. She pulled the book toward her, sucked in a deep breath, and opened it. Air slid from her lungs as she began to read.

The pages were yellowed with age, the ink faded but still

legible. The first page held an unmistakable warning: The cost is irreversible. What you give is gone forever.

Agatha swallowed hard. She turned a page. *Anything. Everything.*

Excitement overtook her, then desperation. She flipped through the brittle pages until she found it—a ritual for restoring life. Her pulse quickened as she whispered the incantation aloud.

Like a nightmare made real, the room shifted as shadows curled and twisted, swooping and dancing around her. The air turned icy and a tremor ran through her fingertips, but she did not stop. She would not—could not. Repeating the words louder now, her voice wavered with pent-up dread, longing, and desperate hope.

A sudden wind gust tore through the room, snuffing out the candle and drowning everything in darkness. Then came the sound—footsteps. Slow. Deliberate. Someone was standing in front of her.

Squinting into the thick, suffocating gloom, Agatha's eyes strained, her breath going shallow and weak. Then, her eyes flew open wide, her heart stalling at the shape that emerged from the dark.

"Agatha," the voice whispered, brittle as dried leaves. It was her mother's voice. She could *feel* her—close, almost close enough to touch.

Trembling, she reached into the murky dark. Her fingers met something cold, dead, hard and unyielding, like graveyard stone. Gasping, she snatched her hand away, but it was too late —her eyes adjusted, and out of the gloom came two faces.

Pale and lifeless, her parents stared back at her, their faces devoid of eyes, their sockets, wide but empty—bottomless hollows that seemed to drink in the light.

The book had worked. The ritual was complete. But something was horribly wrong.

The cold continued, seeping into her bones, devouring every trace of warmth in her body. Agatha reeled, a strangled gasp lodging in her throat as dread curled around her like a tightening noose.

Her parents had returned—but not as she remembered them. These were not the people who once held her, laughed with her, loved her. What stood before her were hollow vessels, their forms warped and soulless, puppets animated by ancient and merciless forces.

And in that instant, Agatha understood. She hadn't summoned salvation and happiness. Instead, she had opened a door that was never meant to be touched.

She had broken something sacred. And the price she had paid—

The reckoning struck her like a physical blow. She had done something vile, irreversible. Heart pounding, she tore up the stairs two at a time, breath ragged with panic. She would beg forgiveness later if there was anyone left to hear it.

The porcelain knob turned with a cold finality, the latch clicking open as she slammed her shoulder against the door. She burst in, screaming her grandparents' names before her gaze drew to their bed and all sanity abandoned her.

Her grandparents lay unnaturally still, their skin tinged with a ghastly blue. Their faces were twisted, locked in expressions of terror, not peace.

Agatha's scream tore from her throat as she reeled, shielding her eyes from the horror she had summoned. The life she knew, warm and full, was obliterated.

There was no one left now—only Danny. The rest she had destroyed with her blind, desperate mistake.

Now to rid herself of her parents.

Rootlings

I n the town of Gable's Hollow, people never discussed the
disappearances. It was considered bad luck. They simply
happened—quietly, inevitably. A farmer may go missing
in the night, or his prize bull, or even a few sheep would vanish
in the early morning hours.

No one called the police. No one asked questions aloud.
They spoke only in low, dread-filled whispers, fearing simply
speaking of the events would bring bad luck or draw the curse
closer to them. Instead, the town's small church would ring its
bell once at dusk, a solitary toll in memory, then the name of
the missing would never be spoken again. That, too, was bad
luck. Most folks acted like this was simply the way things were.
There was nothing to be done except move away or resign yourself to living with nightly terror.

They could leave, certainly. But this valley was very old,
and generations of proud families have called it home since
local records were kept. So, to throw away struggles of all those
who came prior seemed an insult. Too, their lives had not been
easy, and they stuck it out, survived, and thrived.

Ellie Brennan was born and raised in Gable's Hollow. She was still here, even though her mother disappeared when she was five. Her father, who never discussed it, had spent his evenings on the porch with a shotgun across his lap, staring out toward the dense woods bordering their property. He never said what he saw there, but Ellie had learned to sit beside him in silence.

She watched the tree line with him, memorized the hush that fell across the land after dark, and understood from an early age that there were unspoken rules. First, you never went into the woods after sundown. Second, you never mentioned anyone who was missing. Third, and most importantly, you *never* asked what lived beneath the ground.

So, when her father vanished three weeks ago, Ellie told no one. Being a good daughter and being worried of setting the curse squarely on her own shoulders, she kept her mouth shut. There would be no more dinner bells for him. And no one would come knocking on the door to ask questions.

She found his favorite Remington shotgun on the porch, still loaded, still warm. The dog was hiding inside under the table, whining. The only sign of struggle was a set of long, narrow scratches along the floorboards just inside the doorway.

That night, she took the shotgun and sat in the same chair where her father kept watch. She didn't expect answers. She just wanted the thing responsible to try again, so she could be the one to end it.

Six uneventful nights passed. Then, on the seventh, they came.

Ellie had nearly dozed off when she heard it—faint scratching, rhythmic and soft, like claws against wood. After several warning barks, Cord, the young Border Collie, whimpered and hid beneath the couch. Ellie straightened, gripping the shotgun as the scratching grew louder. She ran inside.

The unmistakable sound of wood being pried loose echoed through the house. She spun just in time to see a floorboard shift, revealing a dark gap beneath. To her horror, something began to worm its way through—unnaturally long, pale fingers emerged, blue skin stretched tight over a limb rough as sandpaper, clawing at the air in a desperate search for something to snatch.

Ellie didn't hesitate. Just as Papa had taught her, she firmed up the gun in her shoulder, took aim, and fired.

With an awful screech of pain, the unnatural limb snapped back into the floor, the board falling into place with a clatter. The blast echoed through the house, followed by uncomfortable silence. Even Cord did not dare whimper.

For one glorious, satisfying moment, Ellie believed her defense brought about the end. Then, from beneath the floorboards, came laughter—low, guttural, and full of malice.

Slow realization crept into her mind. The tormenting sound was not a singular voice, but dozens, overlapping, rising and falling in a maddening chorus of whispers, hisses, and choking breaths.

She froze, praying they would not come for her again. Then, unexpectedly, the laughter died as abruptly as it had begun, leaving only the suffocating silence of what remained. Ellie whipped around, staring at the ground as if she could see where they had gone.

"Why did they . . . What . . . How . . ." She spoke to Cord in frantic, broken thoughts, too terrified to organize words.

She ran to the hole and tore at the floorboards where the hand had emerged, expecting a tunnel or a hole. Nothing—just dark dirt. Dry, untouched earth beneath the house. Ellie sat back on her heels, forcing her spinning mind to make sense of what she had seen. None came. Only the terrible realization that she could not do this alone.

"Damn everyone's stupid superstition," she said as Cord, panting happily now, looked on. She ran her fingers through his fur and said to him as much as to herself, "We'll go in the morning."

Cord whined, seemingly happy the threat was gone. For now.

As night fell, Ellie tried to sleep, but every sound brought her to alert. Three boxes of buckshot were on the nightstand. Cord lay curled up on the bed and the shotgun was between them.

Sleep came in fragmented pieces.

———

Dawn finally arrived in its gray glory. Ellie was more tired than she could ever remember, yet things needed done. Mainly, for her survival. Gathering her resolve, she headed outside, crossed the porch, then eased down the steps and out onto the dirt lane. She whistled for Cord to follow, then hoisted the shotgun sling onto her shoulder. He was by her side in an instant, eyes alert, ears catching every sound.

Some twenty minutes later she knocked on the purple front door of Old Mae's house. Mom had spoken of her before, and it was well known she had a long-standing friendship with the mystical woman of the Hollow.

Mae lived alone on the outskirts for as long as anyone could remember. Some whispered she was a witch, which did not bother Ellie at all. In fact, her beliefs were much akin to Mae's way of the world.

When the old woman answered the door, Ellie never had a chance to speak.

"I saw your daddy in a dream," Mae said softly, her eyes shining with an otherworldly wisdom. "He's in the dirt now."

Ellie stiffened, then nodded. "I know you have answers. Those things . . . what are they?"

Mae hesitated, choosing her words carefully. "Rootlings. They live far beneath the land, beneath the trees and stone. Older than the Hollow, older than anyone here. Perhaps even older than humans. This is their world. We are invaders. They are rising up to take back what is theirs. They come at night when the soil's soft and the moon is dark. That's how it's always been."

"Why hasn't anyone stopped them?" Ellie asked. "Why don't we do something? Anything? Call the Army, call the cops, call someone!"

Mae shook her head. "First, you must avoid speaking their name too loudly. Talking about them gives them strength. They will hear." She chuckled. "Humans are ignorant creatures, thinking if they do not talk about the problem, it will go away. In truth, Rootling magic terrifies them. So, we live in fear hoping we are not next."

"Can we kill them?" Ellie fidgeted as they spoke. She pacified herself by squatting to pet Cord.

"Try to fight them and they multiply. That's their defense. Our lowered voices or utter silence are the only things keeping them in check . . . for now."

Ellie's voice dropped. "They already got through my floor. They took my dad and almost got the two of us." She tilted her head toward Cord.

Mae looked her over, then disappeared inside the kitchen. When she returned, she held a jar filled with black ash and something white laying inside—a long, jagged tooth. She pressed it into Ellie's hands.

"Spread the ash in a circle around your house before sundown. Salt the windows. Lock the doors. Never speak to them. Don't look them in the eyes. And don't—whatever you do

—don't go into the woods or fields after dark. Stay in the house until daylight." She pointed to the door. "Go now. Prepare yourself. They will come again."

"Thank you, Mae." Ellie said, resting a kind hand on the woman's shoulder. "I will come find you when this is over."

Mae smiled knowingly. "It will never be over."

After thanking her again, Ellie and Cord headed home to do as instructed. She circled the house with ash, sprinkled salt along the doors and windows, and loaded her pockets with shotgun shells.

For two nights, nothing came. But on the third night, a wind swept through the Hollow, strong and sudden, scattering a portion of the ash circle, the one near the back porch. She noticed too late.

Cord's hackles stood on end as he growled from under the table. He bolted toward the back of the house, barking furiously. Ellie turned just as the door blasted inward.

Rootlings poured in like a swarm—small, twisted things with gangly limbs and pale faces. Their round, hateful eyes were fixed on her. Their mouths were filled with rows of jagged teeth, their jaws snapping as they dashed across the floor.

Cord, his fear gone, lunged, grabbing a single beast by the throat. Growling, he shook it until its neck snapped loudly. The others screeched with wrath and swarmed toward the dog.

"Stay away from him, you filthy bastards!"

Ellie gritted her teeth and fired repeatedly. Each blast hit its mark, sending one hurling from sight or tumbling its broken body across the floor. Shrieking ever louder, more Rootlings scurried forward, swiping at her with razor-sharp claws.

One Rootling latched onto her ankle, yanking hard and throwing her off-balance. She fell into a tangle of biting teeth and clutching limbs, twisting and turning to avoid the worst of their attacks. During their attack, one creature crept closer, seemingly enjoying her panic and dread.

Its breath smelled of earth, mildew, and rotting roots. It leaned in, whispering in a voice like fingers over a chalkboard: "You saw. Now you come below."

"Piss off, shorty!" Ellie jammed the shotgun barrel in its mouth and pulled the trigger.

The creature's head split open like an overripe melon thrown from a window to impact the ground. A moment later the beast—or what was left of it—tipped over in a bloody pile. The others paused, shrieked, then vanished as they had before, melting into shadows and silence.

Ellie lay on the ruined floor, trembling, surrounded by blood and claw marks. Cord came to her side to lick her cheek. She stroked his head.

"Good boy. Good boy."

Cord barked and pushed his head against hers. Ellie lay her hand flat against his trembling body. "I know," she whispered. "I know."

As the sun edged over the eastern horizon, Ellie and Cord went back to Mae's place.

The old woman was sitting on the porch in her rocking chair as if expecting company. "They've marked you now," she said as woman and dog approached. "You're not just a witness. You're part of their story."

Ellie didn't flinch. "How do we end it?"

Mae hesitated, then pointed toward the hills. "There's a well in the old part of town. Boarded up long ago. That's where the soil thins. That's where they come through. It is their home." She went on to lay out a simple plan.

In the end, as she left Mae's house, Ellie understood this was her final chance. If the Rootlings truly hunted her, she would not survive much longer. There were simply too many.

They had to be stopped. An odd feeling of remorse came into her head.

"They were here before us. It's unfair we are forcing them out or killing them for defending their homes. I should have asked Mae that question." Cord barked for her attention. She smiled and rubbed his head. "I know, the little beasts cannot listen to reason. We must stop them."

————

That night, Ellie headed for the well with a rope, her trusty shotgun, a lantern, and the last of the ash.

Pushing down her rising fear, she pried away the boards. She smiled at Cord. "I can't take you, buddy. Wait here. If I do not return, run to Mae's. She will take care of you."

The dog whined for a moment but seemed to understand.

Ellie secured her rope to a thick elm tree, then descended into darkness.

Reaching the bottom, she lit the lantern and found herself in a tunnel—not stone, but dirt. Thick roots curled from the walls like living veins, curling, writhing, seeking. The air was damp and smelled of rain, but the aroma turned sour, filled with death and mold as she walked deeper.

After a while, bones appeared scattered about. Some were small, some adult-sized, others clearly livestock or wild animals. Then she saw the remains of her father's coat, tattered and half-buried in the soil. A dulled ring lay nearby—his wedding band. Kneeling, she gingerly took it up and slid it in her pocket.

"I miss you, Papa. I love you," she muttered. Wiping away the tear forming in her eye, she clenched her jaw and walked on.

A hundred yards later she came to the heart of the creatures' underground kingdom. Rootlings lined the tunnel walls like insects, watching her every move with blank faces. Yet, they did not attack. They simply waited.

Then something enormous stirred in the dark. Taller than any man, its form was a mass of twisted limbs and twitching roots. Dark eyes transfixed on the intruder. It had no mouth, yet Ellie heard it speak, its thoughts and words invading her mind.

"Why are you here?"

"I came to end this."

With a quick motion, she drew her arm back—like hurling the winning pitch of a baseball game—then brought it forward with speed. The jar of ash sailed silently through the air, striking the Rootling's chest.

Like a bizarre, low-budget horror film, the glass shattered— the ash erupting into flame. With a shriek of indescribable agony, the creature ignited, writhing and thrashing as fire surged through the tunnels.

Rootlings joined the chorus of screams, their bodies catching like dry pine needles. The earth groaned and split open. Walls buckled, collapsing behind her.

Ellie turned and ran, shoving the flaming leader aside as she bolted. Reaching the rope just as the tunnel caved in, she kicked off the searching roots clawing at her ankles. Quickly, she hauled herself up with every ounce of strength she possessed, emerging into moonlight as the ground shuddered and split.

In a blink, silence fell thick.

Ellie lay there, panting, staring at the stars as Cord came to her side. She smiled as he licked her face.

Around them, the wind stilled. The well was gone, swallowed by itself.

Long minutes passed before she rose to her feet and headed home. A safe home. A happy home.

In the weeks that followed, no one disappeared. No new names were lost. The town never spoke of what had changed, but the church bell remained quiet, and the lands seemed to have found peace.

Still, Ellie was never far from her shotgun. She bought several more and placed them around the house.

She replaced the broken floorboards and front door. And she never spoke of what she had seen, nor what she had done. When each day ended, she came to bed and fell asleep with relative ease.

But some nights, when sleep would not come, she thought she could hear strange noises again—the faintest sound of scratching beneath the house.

Web of Fear

Mia had always been terrified of spiders. As a child, she would routinely launch herself onto the kitchen table or any other piece of furniture if a spider dared to cross her path. Once, in her haste to escape, she tripped, reeled backwards, and tumbled down the basement stairs, breaking her arm and two fingers in the process.

During those years, as she watched her mother calmly carry the intruders from the house on a piece of paper, Mia could hardly breathe without feeling panicked. Once in a while, her mom would let the furry little beasts crawl on her arm as she toted them outside to 'rehome them,' as she called it. Mia felt sick with fear. She could never understand how her prim and proper mother tolerated being near those awful creatures.

What unsettled her most were their twitching, spindly legs —just watching them move filled her with dread. The clusters of tiny, soulless eyes and the way their slick black bodies caught the light in dark corners made her skin crawl. Nothing else in the world struck her as more disturbingly unnatural.

Over the years, her fear had only grown. She slept with the

lights on, made sure every corner of her room was spider-free, and refused to step into the dark, damp corners of the woods that bordered her house. There were hundreds, perhaps thousands, there, she thought.

But tonight, the night she would finally face her worst nightmare, began like any other.

It was late, and Mia was home alone. Her parents had gone out for the evening, and the quietness of the house wrapped around her like an old woman's shawl. She locked the windows, double-checked the doors, then sat on her bed reading. The dim glow of her Kindle gave her a sense of peace. She felt secure in the familiar cocoon of her room.

Until the sound came. Softly at first, almost inaudible, like a thin strand of hair brushing against her ear. She froze. Then it came again—louder—followed by an unsettling skittering sound just outside her door.

It's nothing. It's just the wind. We are supposed to get rain tonight. I bet it's the storm.

But the sound persisted in abnormal ways, moving, scratching, like tiny feet moving against wood.

Mia's pulse quickened. *Spiders.* She tossed her device aside to fully focus. She could feel their presence, the weight of them hanging in the air. The hair on the nape of her neck stood straight as her eyes darted to the corners where the shadows pooled deeper than usual. The silence of the house, save for the thunder rumbling closer, was complete.

A sudden movement in the corner to her right made her gasp—a shape scuttled across the wall. Too large to be a rat, too fast to be anything else. It was a blur of darkness that anchored her eyes shut in a futile attempt to find a sense of calm. Silence fell again.

Letting her lids drift open, she scanned the room again, terrified of what she might find. Once more, something moved.

Something overhead. Muted with fear, her eyes lifted, her lips parting in horror.

A silhouette, dark and twisted, followed a web strand from the ceiling, stretching out its long, spindly legs with utterly silent motions. It was an enormous spider, one, considering all things, too large not be supernatural in every respect.

Mia suppressed a scream as dizziness weakened her body and fogged her thoughts. A panic attack was edging closer. She felt it. Her vision narrowed and breathing grew rapid.

This creature was larger than anything she had ever seen. But she could not tear her eyes away. She had to look, to face her tormentor. Her upper lip curled up in a disgusted sneer while her heart thundered like the oncoming storm as the beast slowly crept down.

Then it stopped.

Inches above her head, it hung there, suspended like a macabre, oversized puppet dangling from invisible threads. Its legs moving in unnerving fashion. Its body was bloated, black as pitch, with faint red and yellow markings along its abdomen.

No! Please no. Mia's eyes bulged as she stared up. Her body was shutting down while every instinct was screaming to run, to escape the monstrosity. But her mind failed her, blank as a new chalk board.

She could do nothing but watch as her lifelong nemesis' many eyes blinked and bored into her. Two legs clicked. Then it made a sudden, swift leap onto her face.

Mia would have recoiled had it not happened faster than her mind could process. Meaning, her scream never had a chance to erupt from her throat before the spider's venomous fangs sank into her skin.

———

When Mia awoke, her room was gone. She was in a dark, suffocating space where the air was thick and the floor was formed from cold, rough stone. Her skin itched and felt tight, as though something were crawling beneath it, writhing like a sentient being trying to break free.

She instinctively reached out to pull herself upright, but her hands were no longer her own. Now, she felt the subtle movements of multiple legs. Gone were her human hands. Her sleek legs shone black in the dim light. She scrambled to her feet—if she could still call them feet—her body clumsy and foreign. Her eyes saw things in an unusual way, multi-faceted.

Looking down in horror, her eyes fell upon the grotesque sight of eight spindly legs, each tipped with sharp, jagged claws that clicked against the stone. Her body had contorted into something she could never have imagined.

A spider. A very large spider.

Her panic was quickly smothered by primal instinct. Though her mind screamed in terror—the sort beyond the realm of her comprehension—her body no longer resembled the sweet human girl she had once been. Gone were her humanly impulses, replaced by a pull she could hardly fathom.

She felt the urge to crawl, to spin a massive, intricate web, to hide within the shadows, to hunt, and to survive. She could not resist. Slowly moving about the cave in search of an ideal spot, she spied her reflection in a pool of stagnant water. What she saw made her stomach turn.

Her face was hairy with eight eyes staring back. Two central ones for sharp vision, while the others provided depth perception and detected motion. Another pair she felt on the rear of her head enabling her to see in wide angles like early warning sensors, perfectly suited for the monster she had become.

Her beautiful pale skin she had once taken such care of had

become a strange, fur-covered, translucent brown. Her mouth was a gaping maw. She could feel the sharp, gnashing fangs just beneath her lips. Mia would have cried if she could. But all she felt was fear—the overwhelming, inescapable fear that had burdened her for years—now aimed at herself. She had become her worst reality. The very thing she had spent her entire life running from.

With a sudden lurch, she realized something else—her body, massive and hulking, was not alone in the cavern. The walls were lined with webs, sticky and thick.

Dozens of other large spiders skittered over the strands. Several regarded her with cold, calculating eyes as the last vestiges of her humanity died within her new home.

From the shadows, a figure appeared. A massive, monstrous form, its own body a grotesque fusion of spider and man, as if the creature had been born of nightmares, its long fangs glistening, its body covered in thick, writhing legs. The queen approached her slowly. Her presence felt overwhelming.

Something stirred deep within Mia, a pressing urge to kneel, to submit. The queen's multiple eyes locked with hers, and in that moment, Mia understood. This was her fate—to become what she had always feared.

The queen extended a leg, brushing it gently across Mia's new form with reverence.

Welcome to the brood. Long live the arachnids.

And as the darkness closed in, Mia knew there was no escape. No hope of ever returning to the girl she once was. She was caught, bound forever to live out her worst nightmare. The web had claimed her.

Journaling

To any who read this, know I make these pages of my own volition lest I go mad from holding the knowledge inside. Read on and I pray thou dost not judge me harshly. Let forgiveness be set unto me so I may find peace.

May 6, 1837

They believe it began at the edge of the orchard. That is where they found the body, after all. But they are fools—every last one of them. The papers, in their usual way, confessed ignorance, spilling it in columns of ink and absurd speculation. The constables fared no better, grasping at shadows. Even the wide-eyed fools who gathered round my fire, starved for horror, clung to the comforting lie that the girl in the red nightgown—soaked in dew and blood—was the only victim I had ever seen.

But I remember long before that. One night, when the first whisper came in my youthful days, when the wind passed over the fields outside my window, I knew. Knew I was not alone and never would be again.

At first, the whisper was so low I barely heard, but I understood all the same. Outside, the hush between the trees, the stillness in the breath of night, told me things I did not want to hear, edging me toward an irreversible darkness and torturous misery few can comprehend.

People claim to be disturbed by the heinous acts I describe. They lower their voices, shift in their seats, glance around as if the horror might slip from the story into the room itself. But they return. They always return.

Because they do not fear the dark. They fear the part of them that *loves* it.

May 13, 1837

The tavern was never meant for sermons, but that is what its new purpose has become. I have seen to it. My pulpit was a soot-stained hearth. My flock a mix of merchants, whores, wives, husbands, drunkards, and a few quiet souls who listened more carefully than they should.

They named me *The Listener* after I told them about the latest girl. Her death was not printed yet—no announcement, no notice from the constables. And yet I spoke of the cold soil beneath her fingernails. The way her neck had folded when the blade reached the bone.

At first, they laughed. Then they did not.

When her body was found the next morning, people gasped again, wondering how I knew.

That same evening, the room was quieter, but more crowded than it had ever been. Some leaned in through the windows, straddled high ceiling rafters, all while others pressed their backs to the walls, content to stand so long as they could hear the next gruesome tale.

Each story was more vivid than the last. A man's teeth left

on the cobblestones. A woman drowned with her eyes open while staring at her murderer. A young child with a fractured skull and a lullaby still in her ears. Nothing seemed to satisfy their lust for violence or their curiosity.

"How do you know?" they asked.

My reply was always the same. "I listen." What I never told them was *to whom I listen*. I am quite certain they wish to know.

May 23, 1837

The whispers are growing, speaking in low tones I must endure, echoing deep in my mind with a soft but demanding voice most foul. Its awful words are always with me, waiting beneath the clatter of hooves on stone, beneath the creaking of wooden stairs and the shuffling of skirts across floorboards.

It came again after the banker's death. The red-hot poker had entered his chest in clean enough fashion, but the heat set fire to his clothes, making for a horrible, quite odorous mess. Strange how a body can burn so long without making more than a sizzling sound.

His study, which was a truly beautiful room, now reeked of scorched skin. I hear his dog had chewed half his hand like a prime steak cut before anyone found him.

That night, the silence beneath the world hummed louder. It was not only speaking *to* me, I realized, it was singing. An eerie but soothing music.

June 2, 1837

She arrived, as smoke often does—unnoticed until she lingered too long.

Lenora.

She did not drink. She did not giggle or gasp behind a handkerchief like the other women. She did not flinch when I spoke of blood. No, she leaned in.

"What do you *feel* when you tell your stories of woe and death?" she asked after the others had gone. Her voice was low and calm. "Regret? Pride? Terror?"

"None of those, I assure you," I lied.

The truth is complicated. When I tell my tales, when I remember the events aloud, I feel I am laying bricks in a house no one else can see. Each story, each detail, is another wall, another corridor—one I want someone to walk inside and never come out of again.

But Lenora may have seen the door.

I wonder now if she knew where it led.

June 8, 1837

I should have spared him. There was something soft in his face, even as he begged. I cannot even recall why I chose him. Wait, the voices. They picked him. They controlled me. The lad was a candle barely lit. One I was forced to extinguish anyway. My own will is being thrust aside for *them*. I must obey, lest they force my own blade against me, thus ending my usefulness. Perhaps that would be best, I pondered. Yet, I refused to satisfy the hatefulness within me simply by ending it all.

Now, the rocks along the riverbed were slick. Blood makes them worse. Treacherous, really. But it was my own doing, so I have no one to blame but myself. Verily, I cut more than was needed. There was no reason for the second wound—no cause to open the stomach. That was what made the stones so difficult to cross.

But I had felt the burning need to tell such a despicable tale. Killing was merely a means to make it real. A bonus of sorts. The act itself was secondary. What I now craved, what I had grown to love, was seeing the horror and disbelief carved into the ugly, ordinary faces of my listeners.

I do these things not to harm others, but to reveal human weaknesses and frailties in times of deadly crisis. Too, I wish to openly confess to a group of half-wits without being caught. The local police are inept fools who could barely catch a cold let alone hear clues in what is being plainly told to them.

That very night, I spoke of the boy—my latest. As the fire crackled, the listeners leaned ever closer. Lenora said nothing, but her hands clenched so tightly I could see her knuckles whiten. When I said the final line—"His breath fogged the water just once before it stopped"—she stood.

"You were there," she whispered. "You must have been."

I smiled, knowing the truth was far worse. "Surely, you jest and offend me, madam."

That quieted her for the remaining night.

June 16, 1837

Through routine questioning of the villagers, when my turn came, the magistrate thought he could catch me in my own web. Poor fool. He asked about my childhood, my education, my whereabouts on the nights of the killings. I told him stories instead. Stories he did not know were real. I am certain he found me mad. Yet, I convinced him otherwise through lengthy conversations to the contrary.

I suppressed a laugh. The fat man was too ignorant to construct the intricate puzzle I have lain before him. Still, to my delight, he looked pale—near fainting—when they discovered my latest bit of work. Eyes plucked out. Tongue swollen. Scavengers do not cause that. Not naturally.

I did not tell that part of the story, but wrote it here.

Sometimes, I think this book is my true self. My flesh is only the glove I wear to hold the pen.

June 21, 1837

That night, as I told Lenora another story, the tavern was empty. The fire low. Shadows clung to the beams like men hanged for wrongdoings. She sat across from me, still and quiet.

"This story," I said, "is of a man who told stories."

She never fidgeted or even blinked, though when intrigued to a point of excitement, she asked many questions. Most concerned the killer's mindset and feelings. How interesting I found that bit.

On every occasion, I told my stories so well, so vividly, that people mistook me for a messenger. But I was not simply weaving tales, I was remembering. The murders were not visions. They were acts. My own. And Lenora reveled in them, it seemed.

Though, she did cringe, making her forehead crunch tightly as I told her every detail, every thought, every emotion. And how could I not speak of my arousal?

I talked about the orchard. The banker. The boy. The magistrate. The hidden, haunting voices, and more.

"And what happens to the storyteller?" she asked with unusual wonder in her voice.

Our eyes locked. "He meets a woman. A listener like himself. She hears what he hears and understands what must be done."

July 8, 1837

One day, within the walls of my own home, in surprisingly awful fashion, she came from behind me and touched the cold edge of a blade to my throat. I never moved, though a wave of arousal coursed through my body.

"You must be stopped. Today, you've told your last story," she whispered.

I laughed, perhaps giving my final insult if she disbelieved me. "Have I, *partner?*"

July 9, 1837

If you are reading this, if you are still here like the others, then know our story continues.

The ink is still wet. The voices, still speaking, and the music is louder.

And there is so much more to tell. Pay close attention to the words of others, for you never truly know the truth they hold.

Pay the Dead

The funeral was somber. Tears flowed, only to be wiped away with thinly gloved hands or black lace handkerchiefs. Sounds of grieving rippled through the small mourning crowd in the form of incessant sniffling, sobbing, or moaning.

Marcus wanted to vomit, repulsed by the entire proceedings. He was certain nearly all the attendants were the decedent's family. How any rational person could grieve Tony was beyond his comprehension. Even from early childhood, the man had proven himself worthless in every sense of the word. By his twenty-eighth birthday, he had served several prison terms for a laundry list of offenses. Assault, attempted rape, breaking-and-entering, stalking, disorderly conduct, and drug possession, to name a few.

Tony had been a lifelong bully. Unlike many who outgrew their immature ways upon leaving high school, the shitbag, as Marcus called him behind his back, never did. Larger than most, Tony purposely sought out smaller victims for routine humiliation: shoving them in lockers, kicking or punching them, and other unmentionable things. Everyone hated him. Except, of course, other bullies who idolized their leader or women who thought it was a sign of a man to be cruel. But that was all over now. He would never bother anyone again. His life had been snuffed out like a candle flame.

The sole reason Marcus attended the funeral was to pacify his girlfriend, Andrea. Despite his pleas to the contrary, she insisted on paying respects to her ex-boyfriend, an action which only stoked Marcus's anger, especially since she was fully aware of the torment Tony had imposed on him. Yet she seemed disinterested—as if Marcus somehow deserved it.

Simply knowing she had been with Tony was enough to set him on edge. What had she seen in the colossal jerk, he wondered for the umpteenth time.

Nonetheless, he dressed in black and pretended to care about the six-foot piece of crap in the casket, going as far as to shed a few false tears to be convincing. His pride swelled for pulling off the clever deception.

Still, if he had his way, he would unzip his pants and give Tony a belated going away present. The mere idea put a smile on his face, but he hastily wiped it away to display a more appropriate mourning expression. Besides, urinating on the coffin would surely land him in jail.

Then, after what felt like days, the wailing and moaning ceased as the mourners dispersed. Marcus escorted Andrea to the car, being sure to place an arm around her shoulders and whisper lies of his terrible grief.

Once the engine roared to life and he steered his red 1978 Trans-Am onto the road, he felt better. No more pretending, he thought. *Screw that obnoxious slob. I'm glad he's dead.*

Yet he soon realized being glad his tormentor was gone and forgetting him were two different things. The latter hit a snag due to the heavy guilt weighing on his mind.

With Andrea mindlessly staring out the window lost in thought, he replayed the fateful night—an event he hid deep inside. Tony had been standing on his apartment building's roof ledge, high as a kite on whatever drug he had snorted that day. Waving his arms about like an eagle, he said he could fly.

Marcus was only there to beg his tormentor to leave him alone—to stay out of his life, and Andrea's too. But, as it had always been during their school days, he was beaten and laughed at for his fruitless efforts. Battered and bruised, with his ego wilting like a dying flower, Marcus longed to run home and nurse his wounds as he had always done. But then he spotted his chance.

Tony had set up a nearby patio table for his alcohol and drug paraphernalia. All manners of ideas flooded Marcus's mind with glee. Taking a straw and waggling it before Tony's eyes, he coaxed his attacker into snorting another line, then waited.

"Now you're getting smart . . . if that's even possible." Tony smiled before inhaling the powdered white line.

Before long, the big man was solidly stoned—so high he believed he could touch the sun. Those words jolted Marcus to action. He dared Tony to walk the narrow roof ledge from one end to the other. There was no way the prideful fool would back down from a challenge—not even while stoned or drunk, he thought. To seal the deal, Marcus poked at his ego, mocking the ex-football player's ability to pull it off.

After giving Marcus a second thorough berating over his lack of manliness, Tony hopped onto the ledge to perform a surprisingly steady stride.

"Just die, you piece of shit!" cried Marcus, rushing forward to shove Tony off-balance, watching with immense satisfaction as his tormentor tumbled from the ledge, screaming and twisting as he plummeted eight stories to meet the sidewalk with a sudden stop.

In an instant, screams and shouts pierced the air from below. To Marcus, the terrified shrieks were akin to sweet harp music signifying an end to his troubles.

Peering over the ledge as the crowd formed a macabre ring around the dead body, he watched them point, gasp, and wretch. *It's finally over.*

Happier than he had felt in a long time, Marcus proceeded inside, took the elevator to the garage, then drove away as if nothing happened.

To add to his satisfaction, the cops ruled the death an accident. How could they not? Tony's system was filled with a staggering amount of both drugs and alcohol. The case was quickly closed and forgotten.

Andrea's bawling and sniffing brought Marcus back to the present.

"Are you okay?" he asked, using his best concerned voice. Truthfully, her behavior concerned him, not only for her for weepiness, either. Was she edging toward a breakdown? Over Tony? The thought made him sick.

"He was such a great guy," she moaned, dabbing her eyes with a tissue.

Bile rose in Marcus's throat. He wanted to argue—to scream objections over her twisted logic. The urge to shout 'he was a druggie, alcoholic, bully, and general piece of shit. How can you honestly think he's great?' filled his mind. Yet he resisted and nodded an erroneous agreement. "Yep, he was everyone's favorite. What a great guy."

"Just take me home, please. I want to be alone."

Great! I get rid of this arsehole and even from the grave he drives a wedge between me and my dream girl. He would laugh at the irony. Marcus gave another fake smile as he patted her hand. "I understand," he lied. "Shoot me a text tomorrow and we'll connect after you've rested."

Andrea nodded and stared out the window. "I will."

———

Marcus returned to his meticulously cleaned loft, a result of last night's effort. He had done it all in case Andrea might need extra comfort. Even the bedsheets were fresh. As a finishing touch, he sprayed her favorite lavender scent on the linen, knowing it always helped her unwind. Though well aware of her present mood, his anticipation grew, hoping she would seek solace in his arms.

"Well, I have to wait and see what happens." Ambling to his bedroom to change into sweats and a t-shirt, he tried to let the day slip away.

Launching himself onto his bed, he stared out the window, watching the trees sway in the breeze. Birds flitted between branches as thick, puffy clouds sailed overhead, carried by the high wind. Rubbing his face, he exhaled heavily. Restlessness tugged at him, silent but insistent.

Pulling his phone from his pocket, he checked the screen. Nothing. Not a single notification. Andrea had gone silent. The thought irritated him.

He considered texting her, starting a conversation about anything, something to pull her thoughts away from that loser of an ex-boyfriend. But the words would not come.

After a dissatisfied rumbling noise rose in his throat, he gave up and tossed his iPhone on the bed with a huff.

"How can this clown continue to mess up my life? No wonder I hated him." He let the sour words hang, then perked up as the future without his nemesis formed in his mind. "On the positive side, there's a good chance she'll have a full recovery in a week or two. Waiting won't be too bad. We'll get back to normal and put this behind us."

Dragging himself from bed, he shuffled to the kitchen to rummage through the fridge, grabbing two slices of leftover pizza. He tossed them on a plate and stuck them in the microwave.

Hunger was not on his mind, but he ate from reflex alone. Soon, after a bit of video gaming and being bored near tears, he headed back into the bedroom to his calming, clean sheets.

———

Sleep eluded him. Tossing and turning brought no relief. It seemed comfort was beyond his reach. After staring out the window at the drifting clouds and brilliant full moon, he grabbed his phone from the nightstand. Only a lone text from his mother appeared, asking his state of mind after the funeral. He ignored it.

As the screen dimmed and left him in near darkness, strange sounds jolted him. An odd shuffling, followed by the unmistakable creak of floorboards near the living room sofa, echoed in his ears. *Shit! Someone's in the house. I'm being robbed—or worse!*

Startled, he shot upright to squint into the gloom, forcing his tired eyes to adjust. Just then, the passing clouds parted to throw shafts of shimmering moonlight through the dirty windowpanes, illuminating the room in a pale, eerie glow. *There's someone here! It's not my imagination.*

Springing from bed, he seized the baseball bat beside his nightstand and gripped it tightly. Fear drove his heart to the point of exploding. At least, it felt that way as he crept toward the living room.

"Who . . . who . . . who's there?" Bravery surfaced as he

inclined his head sharply toward the front door. "Get out before the cops get here. I'm calling them now." As he edged toward his landline phone to make good on his threat, a deep voice froze him.

"Go ahead . . . murderer," came the graveled reply. "Give them a call. What are you going to say?" The intruder's darkened silhouette shuffled around in a mocking dance. "There's a dead guy in my room. Help me. Help me." He laughed a broken, scratching sound. "Let's see how long it takes for them to haul you away in a straitjacket."

Did he say 'dead'? Keeping both eyes fixed on the darkened shape, Marcus slowly extended his arm to the lamp, switching it on to illuminate the room. He gasped. "No! It can't be!"

With a dread that made his stomach heave, his wide eyes settled on Tony. Despite one side of his head being flattened from impact, one eye dangling from its socket, and blood covering his neck and chest, his tormentor looked the same, save for his shattered right leg. His femur protruded through his jeans, looking quite ghastly.

The bat slipped from Marcus's hands as he reeled with a high-pitched shriek. Pressing his back to the wall, he threw up his arms, bracing as if to fend off an imminent attack.

Tony laughed, but only one corner of his mouth moved. "Always the coward, I see." Moving closer, he lowered onto the couch as if invited over for coffee and a chat.

"Not real. Not real," repeated Marcus, squeezing his eyes shut and sinking to the floor. "He's dead. He's dead."

"Stop repeating yourself. You sound like the same idiot you've always been."

Pushing himself to standing, Marcus shook with fear. "Wh . . . wh . . . what do you want?"

More laughter, a kind that chilled Marcus to the bone,

broke loose from the good side of Tony's mouth. "Payment, of course. You truly are ignorant, aren't you?"

"Stop calling me names or I'll—"

"Or you'll what?" interrupted Tony as his ghastly voice rose. "Will you kill me again . . . murderer?" Intentionally drawing the last word out for the second time, he watched Marcus's reaction closely.

"They didn't bury you this way, right?" asked Marcus, not waiting for a reply or even sure why he asked the question. Fear gave way to anger. "You should be nicely dressed and fixed up." He circled his face with his finger.

"They did, fool," intoned the dead man. "But I wanted you to see what you've done. Bodies inside caskets are only empty shells—façades. Beneath it, I will always look like this." He lifted a bloodied, bruised hand and swept it over his disfigured body. "Just how you made me look. Remember?"

Convinced he was trapped in a nightmare, Marcus's bravery flared. *If he is dead, it doesn't matter what I say. He can't do anything about it. I'll just need to wake up and he'll be gone.*

Marcus straightened and pointed a stiff finger at his tormentor. "You were a worthless human being who took pleasure in terrorizing people. You deserved what you got. And I'm damn proud I was the one who gave it to you."

"Brave words for a little man who needed to fill me with drugs and booze to get the job done." Tony spat, but only a trail of drool slithered down his chin.

Marcus grimaced at the insult. "You did the drugs and booze on your own. I only helped toward the end. Now leave me alone," he cried, seizing the bat again and hefting it.

"Leave me alone," Tony mocked in a child's voice. "Put the bat down, moron. I'm already dead. What are you going to do, kill me again . . . murderer?"

"Stop calling me names!" screamed Marcus, surprised by his ability to confront the man he had feared for years. He lifted the bat higher and bent his knees as if to swing.

"The truth always sucks, doesn't it, tough guy?" Tony chuckled, loosening two teeth, which rolled from his parted lips to clatter on the floor. "I'm here for payment. It's time to pay the dead. Give me what I want, and I'll leave you alone forever."

Imaginary fireworks burst before Marcus's eyes as his fear suspended for a blissful moment. Finally, after years of persecution, the words he longed to hear had come. Secretly, he hoped Tony would not ask for help putting his eye back in its socket or pushing the bones back into his thigh. Though what else a dead guy could possibly want or need eluded him.

"Fine. Name it." Marcus lowered the bat to sit in his favorite chair, hoping the softness would provide some odd comfort as he stared at his homicidal handiwork.

Tony examined his fingernails as if inspecting a recent manicure. "It's simple, even for you. Kill yourself . . . or Andrea. Your choice. *That* is your payment."

With terror forgotten for an instant, Marcus laughed. "And you call me a moron." More laughter.

"Everyone pays their dues eventually. Now it's your turn."

"Ridiculous! I will not harm a hair on her head," retorted Marcus. "I love her. I had to wait for her to dump you so I could have my chance. Now, we're perfectly happy."

"If you say so, lover boy." Tony's loose eye bounced against his cheek as he nodded, reminding Marcus of a grisly rubber ball. One that seemed to stare at him no matter its position. An involuntary retch forced itself toward his lips.

The big man noticed and gave a harsh chuckle. "If you won't kill her that only leaves one option. Go fetch a kitchen knife and finish yourself. Better yet, open the window and take a dive. You know all about high dives, don't you, murderer? Go on, do it now. I want to watch."

"You're even *more* insane than before," spat Marcus. "I won't do it, and you can't make me."

Tony shrugged, his shoulder joints grinding an awful sound. "Fine, dork boy. I'll just pay your sweetheart a visit and explain how *you* killed me. Will she love you then? Who do you think she'll believe?" He ran a hand through his hair. Strands broke loose to fall on the floor. "Poor, pitiful me . . . or you." Pushing his chin at Marcus, he smiled his crooked grin.

Marcus's face reddened in the dim light. "Stay away from her or I'll—"

"Oh, shut up. We've been over this. You're powerless, just like you've always been." Tony let that sink in as Marcus's frame shriveled under the truth. "Now, who's it going to be? Tick tock, tick tock, time is up. Make a choice."

Marcus felt trapped. How could he choose between the girl he had always loved and himself? "I need time to think, damn you," he blurted, hoping to stall for enough time to hatch a plan that would end this all. "Come back next Saturday night. I'll have a decision. You have my word."

"Done." Another tooth skittered across the floor as Tony stood. His thigh bones grated as he rose. "Do the right thing." He drew a finger across his throat and gave another crooked smile. "I'm looking forward to it."

Marcus tried thinking of a snappy comeback, but Tony had vanished. Once more the room sat empty and quiet, save for the steady ticking sound of the small wind-up clock his mother had given him years ago.

"This is absurd," muttered Marcus. "This entire thing was a dream. I have no intention of killing my girlfriend or myself."

Heading to the bedroom to slide under the covers and pull

them close, bat against his chest, he tried to put the nightmare behind him.

———

Wispy clouds drifted high overhead, playing hide-and-seek with the rising sun. But Marcus hardly noticed anything outside his four walls. All he saw was darkness in the form of twisted thoughts as they swirled round, knowing the end result would be a terrible choice he would need to make. Or would he?

"Dead people cannot haunt the living. That sort of thing is merely absurd wives' tales or some movie scene!" His tone was firm in hopes of convincing himself last night was nothing more than an active imagination—a hallucination appearing after a stressful day.

Besides, what *could* a dead guy do? Haunt him forever? Tell Andrea the truth? Would she even believe a ghost—or whatever he was? He considered the awful form in which Tony had appeared. Surely his sweet, innocent Andrea would be overcome with repulsion just by seeing her ex-boyfriend in such a state.

His fingers itched to text her. Should he explain everything before Tony could? *No, it's too soon, especially after saying I would wait for her to heal.* Tossing the phone on his bed, he kept his word and played the long game—patience.

———

Thoroughly discouraged after six days ticked off the calendar and still no word, Marcus could take no more. He snatched his phone to tap the keyboard in frantic fashion, asking to meet

Andrea for lunch. 'It's important.' Within seconds his phone chimed. 'When and where?' she asked.

'Vegan Delight @ noon.' Seconds later, he added, 'Love you and can't wait to C U.' He added several heart emojis, just in case.

'I'll B there.'

Disappointment strangled his pride. "Seriously! She didn't even say she loves me. No little hearts, smiley faces, or anything. Did Tony already visit her?" He smacked his fist into his palm and cursed. "I hate that guy!"

After a hot shower, quick shave, and donning clean clothes, Marcus was as ready as he was going to be. Nonetheless, as he drove to the meeting, each version of the impending conversation made him sound crazier than the last.

"How do I start this?" He paused to let loose a long sigh. "By the way, Andrea, I know this sounds weird, but your dead ex-boyfriend visited me last week and wants me to kill you. Other than that, how have you been sleeping lately?" His palmed his face. "She's going to have me committed."

———

Marcus checked his phone as he sat nervously. *It's nearly twelve. Where is she? The wait is excruciating. What if she doesn't show up? What if she ghosts me and we don't meet before the deadline? What will I tell Tony?*

No sooner had the worrisome thoughts formed than Andrea slid into the booth seat across from him. She looked tired. Her eyes were red as if she had been crying.

"How are you feeling?" he asked from politeness. Inside, he continued to seethe over the haunting fact Tony still held power over her. *She's making my choice easier than I thought. I'm fed up with this nonsense over a corpse.*

"I'm okay," she replied. "Why did you want to meet?"

Perplexed, he almost laughed. "Seriously? Because we're in love. That's what couples do," he said, taking a sip of coffee to keep himself from saying anything he might regret. He wanted to bang his head on the table, maybe even storm out, but knew that wouldn't bring him any closer to a decision. And really, it would just be childish.

And to think I was willing to die for her. Well . . . sort of.

Visualizing an empty seat across from him, he let his head fill with dark thoughts. *How would I plan a murder? Could I get away with it? Wait! What the hell am I thinking? I can't hurt Andrea . . . can I? I mean, it's her or me, right? Or is Tony screwing with me from the grave, making an ass of me one final time? I could go to prison for the rest of my life. No way! I'm getting all worked up over a dream.*

"Are you okay?" she asked.

Marcus jumped at her voice. "Oh, sure. Everything is great," he lied. "Look, I was wondering if you would like to come over tonight. We'll get takeout, watch a movie, and . . . whatever else you want to do."

Andrea's brow creased. "I . . . I don't know."

"Come on. It'll be fun. I miss you and thought we could hang for a bit."

Hanging! I could drug her, then hang her from the support beam in the loft. She would simply go to sleep and never wake up. Painless and perfect. Stop it! I'm not killing her.

She gazed across the courtyard while toying with her napkin. "Okay, I guess so. What time?"

Well, that wasn't exactly enthusiastic, was it? "Let's say seven p.m. Should I pick you up?"

"No. I'll drive, thank you."

Marcus, annoyed into silence, hurried through the rest of their lunch. He could take no more of her depressive state.

After a quick, cold goodbye kiss, they parted. Marcus hurried home to explore how to plan a murder or make a death look like suicide.

———

After thorough internet research, Marcus reached the conclusion he could not kill himself. He hated guns, did not have the courage to throw himself in front of a bus or out the window, and hanging himself was definitely out. All that kicking and flopping around while struggling for air was a turn off. And he certainly could not poison himself. The remaining choice was becoming perfectly clear.

To his surprise, he discovered several interesting ways to rid himself of his lover. Some belladonna herb in her drink would do the trick nicely. Shoving her down the building's broken elevator shaft would work, but he worried over being seen by the security cams. Plus, if he finished her off in his loft, ridding himself of the body was a real concern.

Shoving her in front of the subway train or downtown bus were both viable, but those blasted security cameras ruined those ideas, too. It would take too much time to discover their blind spots and formulate a viable plan without being seen. Tony would be back before then.

Marcus was still deep in thought when the doorbell rang. In an instant, all his plans evaporated. He would have to improvise.

After a curse, he slapped shut his laptop, then straightened his clothing before answering the door. At least he had showered and changed clothes since lunch. *If I'm going to kill her, she should at least remember me this way.*

Andrea brushed by him to sit on the couch. Marcus held up a glass. "I've got your favorite wine chilling. Want some?"

She nodded as she fiddled in her handbag. "That sounds great." Her eyes lit up as she found her prize. "I have something for you." She sounded perkier.

Marcus noted the change. His hopes for a romantic evening and setting their relationship back on track were rising. "Awww, that's sweet." He set two full glasses of red wine on the table. *Maybe she has finally left Tony behind. Hell, it's been long enough.*

Half the glass passed Andrea's lips within a half hour. Loosening up, she moved closer to massage his thigh. Leaning in to kiss him, she was met with both fervor and enthusiasm. Her hand found his crotch, putting all thoughts of her murder out of his mind.

Marcus tilted his head as their tongues danced for several blissful moments until sudden pain overtook the joy of her warm touch. He jerked upright, pulling away from her embrace, uncertain what had happened.

Each breath fell short. Pain radiated through his body. His surroundings dimmed as a chilling cold plunged him deeper into darkness. Dropping back against his favorite fluffy cushion, his head tilted to one side as his life force drained away, flowing over his stomach and groin.

With questioning eyes, he stared at Andrea as she slid the thin knife from between his ribs. She wiped the blade clean on his new pants, gazing on with a remorseful face.

"I'm sorry, baby. But it was you or me." She shrugged. "Tony told me it was the only way I could be with him again."

Only gurgling noises rose from Marcus's lips as his outstretched hand dropped away.

"Great job, lover," said Tony, appearing near the balcony doors. He swung them open. "Now it's your turn. You know I can't come back to your world, but you can join me here."

"Hold on." Andrea stood up, gazing between both men.

"Won't Marcus be there, too? We'll all be stuck together. I don't want to go through this again."

Tony laughed. "I'm sure he went somewhere else. We'll never see him again."

"How do I know I'll find you in the next world?" she asked, moving to the railing and peering over the edge before backing away, looking pale.

"Have I ever let you down?" His words glided out with a subdued slyness.

Andrea studied the street below as fear and doubt registered on her face. "No, I guess not."

"Now it's your turn. Come on. Get it done. Join me, sweetheart," he prodded.

Andrea shook her head, turning to back away. "I can't. I won't."

Tony blocked her. "Baby, don't be like that." His ghastly expression changed. "I might as well tell you: I never loved you anyway. You cheated on me and deserve whatever you get. Now jump before I throw you."

She clapped both hands to her ears. "No! It's not true. You love me. And I . . . I . . . Marcus was just so nice, and he was sweet. Why did you make me kill him?"

Tony laughed his grating sound. "I didn't make you do anything." He stepped closer and waved a hand, losing a finger as it broke free to land at his feet. "Take another look. You'll see how easy it is."

Andrea hesitantly peered over the railing's edge again to take in the concrete far below. She swallowed hard and again tried to back away. But Tony stood in her way.

"Say good night, my little cheater," he said, shoving her hard, watching her legs spin past his face as she plummeted over the edge toward her death.

As if watching a replay of his own demise from a different

86

angle, Tony observed the crowd quickly gathering round with their shrill shrieks and terrified screams. Phone camera flashes lit up the night like exploding stars.

Tony laughed. "You two idiots were made for each other." Another deeper laugh. "Revenge is soooo sweet." He faded away, leaving Marcus dead on his couch and Andrea's body in a widening pool of her own blood.

The detectives closed the case quickly, convinced of a murder-suicide. After all, there was no proof to the contrary.

An Affair

Darkness prevailed. Still, even in the cool of night, I perspired. Digging is laborious work regardless of the hour. Gregory, my longtime friend, lay next to me swathed in heavy canvas, tightly secured by means of thick rope.

Earlier this evening, we exchanged harsh words after he arrived in a rage, accusing me of bedding his wife with unrestrained frequency. During our squabble he lunged at me in anger, his right hand connecting with my jaw. His powerful blow sent me to the floor in a heap.

Alas, the days of dueling have fallen from fashion, or pride would have compelled me to demand satisfaction in such manner. Since he wounded both my dignity and person, his attack could not go unanswered. The only question was how.

Maintaining my gentlemanly manner, I dusted myself off, then slyly calmed his anger by offering to ply him with alcohol. Knowing him as I do, I was keenly aware strong libations were his weakness. The poor sot was prisoner to mortal vices, continually overindulging his nasty habit. Around town he was known for being just short of a constant drunkard, albeit a wealthy one.

We reminisced for some time over our friendship. We had grown up together and had countless adventures to look back upon. In school, we were best mates. Of course, there had been the normal rowdiness and mischief one expects from teenaged boys, and there were phases of smoking, drinking, and whoring as we grew older. Our time together gave me pause for what I was about to do, but a price must be paid for his foolishness. In hindsight, I was going to truly miss him.

After watching him empty his fourth glass of my finest liquor, I lead him onto the balcony with the pretense of admiring tonight's full moon. There, still fuming over the physical thump he gave me, I waited until his back was turned, then seized a small granite garden statue and struck him from behind. Ironically, the weighty decoration was that of Venus, the goddess of love. Should he still be alive, Gregory would have found amusement in that small quirk of fate.

Nonetheless, my delivered blow carried force enough to open his skull like a ripe melon, driving his left eye from its socket to launch over the balcony's edge like a morbid shooting star. Two teeth burst from his mouth as his face impacted the cement railing.

Having no reason to search for the missing fleshy orb since, undoubtedly, a raven or some such wild creature will feast on it, I retrieved his incisors to pocket them, making a mental note to include them in his grave.

For a long moment, I stared at his disfigured head but soon turned away after it was clear he would not move again. I will admit it was a ghastly sight, yet I felt no remorse since the cruel deed needed done to regain my honor.

Here, I pause to confess. Each allegation he presented was true. I indeed lusted after his wife, Charlene, for some time.

She is a wonderous, pale-skinned beauty with luscious raven-colored hair and round emerald eyes. Average in stature and steady in demeanor, she bears a dignity and lightness to her steps. Her voice brings joy with its airy quality, as if a living fairy speaks to you. For years she had rebuked me, until one glorious day she invited me into her arms. That was many months ago.

Unfortunately, our current woes began after we were foolish enough to believe our meetings were secret. We were wrong. Somehow, Gregory discovered us. Personally, I suspect the maid informed him of my frequent house visits.

Back to my present situation, murder is a far messier business than one would believe. Furthermore, hiding the small traces of said act is even more difficult. Thankfully, Gregory was gracious enough to lay quietly in wait as I cleansed the site of his untimely demise. Soon after, and with great effort, I transported his stiffening body to the woods, placed him neatly off to the side, then dug his eternal resting spot before sliding his corpse into the deep hole.

Presently, that is all I can say on the matter. At least, all that could be written. As my recollection ended and I set pen and paper aside, exhausted to my bones, gray light streamed through the rose-shaped window. Here in the comfort of my favorite chair, pipe in one hand and whiskey in the other, I thought the time for rest had come. But the luxury of sleep was not to be mine.

The light clopping of horse hooves over the hard dirt lane gave me a welcomed rush. Watching through the window as Charlene's carriage arrived early, I set aside my things and hurried outside to meet my lover. After stowing her conveyance and turning her fine team of horses out to pasture, I rushed to her side. Minutes later, and much to my delight, we engaged in a long, vigorous lovemaking session.

We spent time on the veranda overlooking the cool, darkening forest on this fine evening. We drank wine, laughed, melted into one another's arms, and renewed our excitement of love. She always had a way of making me blush by recounting the way we had met and the thrill of sneaking behind Gregory's back for our tender meetings.

Quite satisfied with ourselves after our second sexual encounter, we dressed and proceeded to the kitchen where the story of her husband's demise spilt from my lips like water over a fall's edge. I could not stop it. Though I held no reasoning for revealing the truth, the words forced themselves out as if my actions were not my own. The more words that passed my lips, the greater satisfaction I derived.

At the conclusion of my tale, it felt as though a great mental weight was lifted from my shoulders. I anticipated her joyous reaction. After all, it meant we could be together forevermore, free of Gregory and his drunken stupidity. Alas, like my sleep hours earlier, I was a fool to believe such an outcome would be.

"Fool! Idiot! Why did you kill him?" she shouted, shaking her fist at me. "You had no right to take him from me. His wealth kept me in fine clothing and jewelry. Far more than you could ever give. You think I do not know that for all your fancy belongings you are nearly penniless? You could never give me the life I desire."

Flummoxed, I lacked a response for several long moments. "Did you not hear me? The buffoon stained my honor," I countered in confusion more than anger. "You need not fear, my love. I hold more than enough wealth to keep us happy. Now we can truly be together."

She laughed before narrowing her gaze and turning grim. "Jester! You helped me pass the time during Gregory's business outings. Nothing more. Your moronic misdeeds have ended our arrangement. I will see you hang for this. Besides, I have other lovers, ones better than you, who will keep me amassed in riches and pleasures of the flesh."

Akin to the physical blow I had received earlier, my face grew warm with anger. Fury boiled in my heart. *How dare she use me so callously, then toss me aside. Was it true? I had been nothing more than a dalliance. Someone to fill her long nights and warm her bed? The nerve of the wench was boundless. Clearly, I loved her more than the others.* Still, ever the gentleman, I attempted to reason with her again.

"You . . . you no doubt speak from wrath. It will pass, my love," I stammered.

"My love!" she screamed, pointing a stiff finger at me. "Never say those words to me again."

Seizing the fruit bowl from the dining table, she hurled it at my head, followed immediately by a brass goblet and several pieces of silverware. I avoided most, but one sharp paring knife imbedded itself in my forearm. With a howl, I pulled it free as blood ran to drip from my fingertips. My tempered anger released, quickly spilling over into animalistic abandon.

Knowing she had stirred me beyond rational judgement, her eyes shot wide as she turned to flee. I pursued her down the dark, wood-lined hall before bursting out the front door. Ahead lay the wide, green lawn, fresh and dewy.

As we ran, I drew closer to her with each step. Reaching the tree line, I dove with open arms to tangle in her feet, then sprang atop her, straddling her chest. I slapped her hard. She gasped at the impact as her cheek reddened, and a dribble of blood escaped the corner of her mouth.

Bucking and squirming, she thrust her hips upward and drove her knees into my back, unbalancing me for an instant. In a quick motion, she grabbed a stout, fallen tree limb and pummeled my temple, dazing me to the point of a stupor.

With a groan, I fell to one side as she leapt away to sprint into the forest. Dizzy and bleeding, I gave chase, wiping away the warm crimson liquid as I went. My eyes could not refocus immediately, forcing me to rely on other senses. I paused to listen, catching every bird chirp and chipmunk chatter. To my left, dried branches snapped, and leaves rustled. I lingered long enough to wipe the blood from my eyes, then ran toward the sound.

"Charlene!" I cried repeatedly. No answer. "Come, I shall explain."

My throbbing lacerations made it difficult to muster a degree of logic, as did the overpowering anger and injustice I felt from her cruel rebuke. As such, it was not hard to deduce the only appropriate outcome for her was to join her husband. After all, that *is* what she wanted.

I searched the grounds, my gaze roving here and there. A small, momentary sighting would be all I need to snare her. The surrounding woods were my home, and I knew them well. She could not—would not—escape.

To my dismay, it seemed Charlene had vanished from view. During my search, she must have circled back from whence she came and now bolted toward the stables. It took several precious seconds for me to comprehend her intentions. Realizing where her current path would lead, I hastened along, my legs powering me forward on a much shorter route, one unbeknownst to her.

I arrived first, a mere minute before she cautiously emerged from the forest. Even while moving with care, she would cover the distance quickly, so I hurriedly searched for a weapon. Halters, ropes, saddles, and more useless things hung about. Then, in the corner, I saw my chance in a pitchfork. I seized it, hid myself close to the entrance, then stood in wait. *See me hang, will you? I think not, treacherous strumpet.*

I hunkered down, coiling my body and squaring my feet,

ready to lunge. It would be over in a moment, but a curse sprang from my lips as fate turned her toward the house. When she did not waver from it, I followed at a sprint, pausing to peek from behind the massive oak tree trunk in the front yard. Dashing on, I concealed myself behind the neatly groomed shrubs, watching closely.

Her shoes grated the dirt drive as she unwittingly shuffled my direction. The pitchfork hefted higher in wait. I stood stone-still in anticipation. But then, caught up in a tempest of haste and anger, I rushed after her for an ill-timed attack with the tines leveled at her heart. Seeing my seething rage, she yelped, made the short dash to the house, then slammed and bolted the heavy front door. Undeterred, I made for the unlocked side entrance.

Entering the kitchen, I abandoned my unwieldy weapon, placing it softly on the counter to retrieve a large knife from the block. Creeping over the hardwood, I cursed, hitching my breath with each creak and moan of the boards. My footsteps lightened, my weight balancing precariously on the balls of my feet as I snuck down the short passage to round the sharp corner leading into the den.

Charlene was suddenly before me. I lashed out instinctively, my blade opening a gash on her forearm. She shrieked, standing frozen for a long instant that rendered me still as well. Then, with a motion faster than expected, she retaliated. Aiming the fireplace poker at my skull like splitting wood with an axe, she swung to connect in brutal fashion.

Fortunately, quick reactions saved me from a more serious predicament, though the end result was not fully to my advantage. The iron glanced off my temple, continued downward to make a significant wound on my ear, then impacted my collarbone with vigor. I cried out as the thin bones gave way with a dreadful snapping sound. My left arm fell to my side in limp fashion.

Stunned and reeling about in agony, I crashed rearward, landing atop a low table to send a shower of wooden splinters into the air. From my back, I scrambled to my knees, fighting for a semblance of balance as she moved toward me, the poker held high.

My right hand hurriedly rummaged through the jagged debris in search of my knife, ignoring the slivers that tore at my skin. Finally, the knife's wooden handle slipped into my palm. I grasped it tightly as her next stroke came with speed. Lurching to one side, I barely avoided the powerful swipe while luckily glimpsing an opening to strike. I slashed again, this time contacting with her thigh to open another nasty cut.

Pressing my advantage, I struggled upright and lunged at her for a final blow. To my disbelief, it went astray. Conversely, hers did not. This time her poker connected with my knee, dropping me back to the floor. I howled in pain, growing dizzy from agony and blood loss as she escaped again, seemingly unaffected by her wounds. My grunts morphed into curses, which soon fell silent.

It was odd. Why did she not end my life here and now while the opportunity presented itself? Could her amorous feelings remain, and our troubles prove merely a misunderstanding? New hope took root within my heart. Perhaps she still loved me.

A shake of my head displaced the ridiculous thought. Hauling myself upright by means of the thick, wooden desktop, I straightened, dusting off my clothes before pursuing. Though I silently confessed amazement at her spirit and valiant resilience, I knew it was time to end the hunt.

Each step brought suffering as the impact jarred my swollen knee. Coupled with the slightest arm movement from my left side, the actions formed tears in my eyes. I felt awkward and clumsy, not traits I desired while planning to confront an able-bodied, angry woman wielding a lethal weapon.

Passing the hearth to move to the window, I drew back the curtains to flood the room with light. Running the sharp blade across the hanging fabric, I hurriedly constructed a makeshift sling. Bile rose in my throat as the loop went over my head. The pain was excruciating, yet there was no option but to bear it and pursue.

Onward I went, as my disposition worsened. No longer did I wish to slay her quickly and lay her next to her husband. Instead, I yearned to make her writhe in pain in similar fashion to my own. She had broken both my heart and bones. She had driven a blade, both physical and intangible, inside me. As such, I would do the same to her.

Hoping to strike fear in her heart and trusting she would cower at my approach, I called her name again. "Charlene! I have a gift for you. Come hither, my sweet! Bless my eyes with your beautiful presence."

I heard neither breathing nor movement. Where had she gone? Then, the barely perceptible sound of a closing door came from the hallway. Hoping my one good ear had not played a vile trick on my imagination, I hurried along.

Starting with the closest door, I took the knob firmly in hand and twisted ever so slowly. Locked. To be sure it was not a mere ruse I pressed my good ear against the wood. Inside was quiet and still. I moved to the next, repeating the procedure and was met with the same results until I stood before the final pair of doors. One stood before me and the other was to my back.

I wriggled the handle hard. Though locked, I heard a glorious sound. Charlene's gasp, terrified and pitiful. The sound delighted me.

"There you are, my little angel. I hear you," I cried before throwing my weight against the wood. "I am coming, my sweet love. You may join Gregory yet."

Each jarring blow weakened my knees as pain ripped at my aching muscles. The sling held steady yet could not relieve my agony. Vomit rose, but I fought it down and slammed myself against the door again.

When my shoulder would stand no more, I backed away to kick repeatedly until the frame began to splinter. For a final time, I threw my person against the door. The wood broke away to swing the door wide as I sprang inside.

"No!" I screamed upon realizing the room sat empty. Thwarted again. Though this time, there was little guessing as to the means of her escape. The wench had crawled out the window, which was flung wide, leaving the curtains moving in the gentle breeze. I hastened to it to spot her fleeing across the lawn, heading toward the barn in another attempt to retrieve a horse from the pasture, which lay on the western side of the structure.

I hobbled back to the hall, stumbling round the corner as I headed for the back door. Bursting through, I ran as best I could, grimacing as the hard ground abused my body. I fought the onslaught of nausea caused by the incessant throbbing of my wounds.

For a moment, some fifty feet separated us, but I quickly closed the distance as her wounded leg slowed her more than she knew. Too, her lengthy dress was a welcomed hindrance.

I was not alone in my thinking as she, mid-stride, ripped and tore at its length, leaving tattered pieces as a trail of sorts. Still, it did little to prevent my advantage. My knuckles whitened around the knife handle. Time to pay was nearly upon my once-beloved Charlene.

Ten feet. Five. Two. I lunged to grab a fistful of her hair, which had fallen loosely round her shoulders and lay far down her back. With a hard yank, I jerked her from her feet to land in a painful spill as our frames intertwined and tumbled about the lawn.

Again, overwhelming pain took me as I thumped to the ground. The knife flung from view, lost as my eyes squeezed shut in agony. A heave burst from my lips. Fighting to clear my vision, I rose wobbly, only to have her shin impact my groin with another round of mind-numbing results. The sound of tearing resumed as I collapsed. Forcing my eyes open, I saw only strips of her dress at my feet. Meanwhile, her light foot-falls, the ones I had previously adored so, rushed over the soft grass as she returned to the house.

Again, the questions bit at me. Why had she not continued to the horses? Was her wound of such she could not mount her stead? It mattered not. Our little game was becoming tedious. Shameful, even. I knew, as I lay there bleeding and sobbing, that I could not maintain this vigor much longer. This woman had harmed me beyond any personal limits I dreamed possible.

Driven by mounting vehemence, I hurriedly recovered my knife, tucked it into the back of my breeches, then ran for the kitchen door, staggering and weaving as I went. Deeming she would be close by in the little time that had passed, I bolted inside, believing she could not have already prepared an ambush.

I should have sensed something was afoot when the door proved no barrier, but in anger I raced ahead. Suddenly, a soft, lilting voice rose behind me. I faced her with a false smile, but it was for naught. As she had several times that night already, she stepped closer, and with a swift motion, hurt me again. This time was much worse than before, though I did not know at first what she had done.

My vision went hazy, and my legs no longer held me. I tipped over, landing on my back to stare at a long wooden stick that appeared to grow from my chest like a small, lovely tree sapling. My brain disallowed me from making sense of the image as a wave of coldness swept over my skin, raising goosebumps as mental clarity faded.

Smiling with glee, Charlene placed a foot on my shoulder and gave a jerk, freeing the pitchfork from my chest. Life drained from me like water from a spilt glass. Coughing up blood, knowing she had wounded me to death, I attempted one final trick.

I curled my finger to draw her close, pretending to impart one final thought before I would breathe no more. She hesitated as I continued to beckon. I knew my time was short.

Finally, she gave in. Whether from sorrow or arrogance, I would never know. As she bent closer, her hair fell forward to caress my face—a glorious feeling to die with, I thought. Then, I freed the knife hidden behind my back and with my remaining strength, plunged it through her breast.

She sucked in a quick breath. Her eyes shot wide, then lowered to stare at the protruding blade.

The gleam in her eyes, once silently announcing pride and satisfaction as I struggled to take another breath, dimmed. She collapsed on my chest in an odd sort of farewell embrace before uttering my name and reaching to stroke my face with feeble fingers.

Then the gods took us, and we were no more.

Concussion

I'm dying. So, before I lose consciousness, I will transcribe my entire story from the beginning. Maybe you will learn from it.

First, I'm not crazy! Even though these events may sound like something from one of R.L. Stine's *Goosebumps* books, I assure you every word I write is true . . . I think.

Before coming to Willow Grove one fine sunny day, I fell down a flight of stairs. No, I'm not clumsy. I just had my arms full while carrying a large box, couldn't see the steps very well, and the next thing I knew, the box was in the air and I was ass-over-teakettle, as my grandpa used to say. Down I went, all thirteen stairs pounding my body, breaking my nose in the process.

You know, maybe thirteen really is unlucky. Anyway, the confusion, slightly slurred speech, and dizziness started shortly afterward.

Doc Marsden said I'd be fine if I rested for a while. She told me to take a week off to relax. I was to avoid reading, texting, gaming, and loud music. Which is perfectly fine since I hate loud music and am not a gamer, so no loss there, but I do love to read and text. Those two were very hard to give up.

I wasn't supposed to drive either, but that bit of advice I will skip. I would go nuts sitting here with nothing to do for an entire week.

I had no idea where to go so I pinned a state map to the wall, closed my eyes, and tossed a dart. I'm heading for Lightning Lake. That's my destination. Great, that part is done.

After an hour of online research, I found the perfect cabin and rented it for an entire week, just like the doc said. I won't ever tell her I did not follow her instructions to the letter. Besides, I feel fine, except for the growing headache I hope to manage.

Packed and ready, I headed out, arriving here four days ago. I'll admit, the drive was painful.

Here, I have no internet, no cell service, and no television, per doctor's orders. And not one damned book in my possession. Hoping I did not go from one bad situation to another, I realized I may just as easily go crazy from boredom here than at home. Oh, how wrong I was.

Strange shit started happening on the first day. I arrived after a four-hour drive and pulled into the service station to fill my tank. Doc warned me about light sensitivity, and even with my dark sunglasses the sunshine felt overpowering. My head was officially killing me.

I rubbed my temples, then snatched a bottle of Excedrin from my backpack. Grabbing up my fancy steel water bottle, I washed the white pills down in one gulp. Dizzy and growing rather grouchy, I fumbled with the gas hose, hoping I wouldn't burn the place down in some freak accident just because I couldn't concentrate. I pushed the nozzle into the filler and squeezed the handle. The cursed pain was crippling.

Instead of watching the meter, I grabbed the folded map from the passenger seat to lay it over the hood, then tried to study the colored lines. It was tough. Everything was blurred. "Shit!" I hollered. Fuzzy vision, another unwanted side effect. I know, I wasn't supposed to read. But how else was I going to find the cabin?

Taking a deep breath, I calmed myself. Doc said I needed to avoid stress and have quiet for a few days before slowly ramping back up to normal. Whatever normal is, I thought. I folded the map and tossed it back onto the seat. What good was it if I couldn't read it? Ignoring doc's advice seemed dumber with each passing second.

The nozzle clicked off. I replaced it, then moved toward the front door of the convenience store. And since I needed to get good directions anyway, why not pay inside? I thought it was the logical choice.

Inside, a few people meandered about, but as my eyes met the attendant I sucked in a quick breath. I reeled, backing into a shelf, nearly knocking the entire thing over. Trying to look as though I planned it, I adjusted my Life Is Good cap and dark shades. "Sorry about that," I offered while straightening things up.

No response came. I took another look. There was no person standing there. Instead, it was some weird monster. I shit you not. This thing looked like it belonged in an old-time horror film. The Creature from the Black Lagoon springs to mind.

Well over six and half feet tall, its gill slits moved in rhythmic fashion as it breathed. Long clawed fingers were joined by webs. It had shark's eyes: black, large, empty, and perfectly round. With skin akin to fish scales, I wondered how it survived away from water. Maybe it didn't even need water.

Hell, maybe it drinks blood or motor oil or some other weird shit to stay alive.

Just as that thought formed, the creature picked up a spray bottle and spritzed itself about the face and neck. So that's how it does it, I thought. What is it? Where did it come from? Can anyone else see it? Why are they not freaking out? Or do they know and just keep quiet about it? I mean, there were a half-dozen other people in here, too. Yet I was the only one seemingly aware of the monstrosity among us.

My head throbbed horribly but I couldn't tear my eyes away. I was terrified to move closer, but there was little choice. I had to pay for the gas and get directions.

Swallowing my fears, I steadied myself, trying to act ordinary. Within four steps I doubled over in pain. It felt like my eyes were bulging out of their sockets. Once I straightened, my gaze returned to the clerk. This time there was a tall, thin, handsome young man standing there. Long black hair hung over both shoulders and his dark eyes met mine.

"Are you okay, mister?" he asked.

"I . . . I . . . yes, I'm fine. But I'm a bit lost."

"I've lived here all my life. Where ya' headin'?"

"To an Airbnb I rented for a week." Without averting my eyes, I fumbled in my pocket to pull out the directions I printed before leaving home. "237 Cottonwood Road. House #5." I pointed to the paper.

"Sure, I know it. The Orwell's have five cabins up there. You picked a great spot. There's no traffic either. You'll enjoy it." He pointed to the main road. "Head out of town. Go north for about two miles and you'll see a huge sign on the right. It says, 'Cabins for Rent.' Turn there, go another half mile down the dirt lane and you'll be there. Easy peasy."

I held back a laugh. Does anyone even say 'easy peasy'

anymore? Great, not only is some damned alien giving me directions, but I'm in Hicksville, USA, too.

Another stabbing pain rocked me, turning the laugh into a grimace. Fumbling to free my wallet, I dropped it. Embarrassed, I stooped to pick up my mess. My credit cards had skittered across the floor and several ten-dollar bills floated through the air like birds taking flight. I cursed several times in my head.

Then, a sudden, agonizing jolt rocked me. I squeezed my eyes shut. As I opened them again, I saw a leathery clawed limb coming toward me.

"Mister! Mister! Should I call 911?"

Does Hicksville even have 911 service? Grimacing, I shook my head and waved him off. "No, no, I'm fine. Just an awful headache." We made eye contact again as Black Lagoon boy spritzed himself once more. I looked away and shut my eyes, doubting my own vision.

Just make him go away. Go away, go away, I silently repeated. I raised my face and slowly cracked open my eyelids. They flung open wide as the dark-eyed young man raised a water bottle to his lips and drank as if nothing had happened. Is that what I had seen? Not a monster trying to stay hydrated, but a thirsty kid who likely thought I was a nut job. Was this all a figment of my imagination? Maybe he *should* call 911.

Composing myself, I gathered my belongings, paid for the gas, then hustled back to my ride. I couldn't resist taking a backward glance. Sure enough, Lagoon boy had moved to the door and was waving goodbye, his webbed hand swishing back and forth like a duck paddling water. A fresh sheen of sweat broke over me and I turned away, almost running across the station.

"None of it is real. It's not real," I muttered as I went.

Back in my car, I fired up the engine and hit the road with screeching tires. What the hell was happening? Was Doc right? She did say I could hallucinate, especially if I overloaded my senses. And the woman was a genius: a great doctor. I trusted her every word. Or I *should* have. Maybe the trip was too much. But I couldn't turn around now and face another four hours on the road. That would make things a hell of a lot worse.

I rolled through town, heading north as Lagoon boy instructed, and everywhere I looked, they were there. The tourists, hikers, and campers were easy to spot. They stuck out like clothed, white flesh sausages with feet. But others, the residents I assume, were horrors. No two were the same. I saw tentacled arms, fur-covered bodies, sharp fangs, limbs that dragged the ground, or swishing antennae poking from high, red foreheads. They were everywhere. Dozens strolled the streets or sat in cafes eyeing the passersby. And that meant me. Did I look like a freakin' snack to these things?

A shiver raced down my spine. Terrified in ways I had never dreamed possible, I looked left. One sasquatch-sized furry beast with four arms sprang from an alleyway to swing a huge limb through the air. His victim, a balding, plump little man, waddled past with a backpack strapped over his meaty shoulders. He looked like a lost a five-year-old on a school trip.

The poor dude never saw it coming. His chunky body took the full blow. The impact drove him forward with incredible speed, crunching his face against the sidewalk, spraying blood over the pavement in every direction.

"Holy shit!" I screamed. Thankfully the windows were up as I stomped on the brakes to watch in disbelief. In a quick motion, the creature bent to seize the man's ankle, hoisted him up like a ragdoll, then brought him down repeatedly, pounding him into a jellyfish-like status. Each thump brought a sick crunching sound. The creature tossed the broken body to his right to land against a stone bench, bloodied and twisted as the fat hiker's dead eyes stared straight at me. Bile rose in my throat. I wanted to vomit.

Sasquatch leapt onto his victim to tear their limbs away as easily as a human peels a banana. More blood filled the air like rain.

"What the hell is happening!" I shouted again, glad the windows were up. "Why is no one else seeing this!"

Trying desperately to make sense of my vision, I turned in my seat to stare at the others who simply strolled along, oblivious to the ghastly murder taking place twenty feet away in plain view.

The carnage did not stop. Two doors down, a woman gazed in the window of The Doughnut Hole, a local pastry shop. I trembled in stunned silence as a dark blur passed by at incomprehensible speed. Just like that, she was gone. The impact from the werewolf drove her out of her Birkenstocks, which remained firmly in place on the sidewalk. Her shouts of pain and terror rolled down the street, piercing the day with the feel and sounds of death.

"Make it stop," I hollered. Yet people took no notice. They strolled about without so much as a batted eyelid. "Maybe I'm losing my mind. Maybe it's a tumor," I stuttered to myself before displacing the thought. The doctors would have found it, either in the CT scan or MRI. They said I received a clean bill of health. But my version would explain a lot.

Almost against my will, terrified of what I might see, I looked across the street once more. Sasquatch and his victim were gone. In their place were two large men sitting on the stone bench, feeding the pigeons congregated at their feet. Smiling and chatting, they dug into their bags to toss birdseed onto the ground. A dozen birds cooed happily around them.

Back to The Doughnut Hole. The woman's fancy footwear was absent with no signs of the brutal attack visible. In her spot now stood a mother and son. The young lad pointed at a tray of chocolate-covered pastries in the window and could barely contain his excitement. He hopped from one foot to the other. The mom laughed as they opened the door to step inside and disappear.

Frightened and confused yet sure of what I'd seen mere moments ago, I was ready to bolt. I threw my vehicle in gear and mashed the gas pedal to the floor. I took to the road in a cloud of dust with the sound of squealing tires rising behind me. If I stayed any longer, I would be the next victim. It would be just my luck to be eaten here in Hicksville.

Minutes later, the sign Lagoon dude mentioned grew larger as I sped toward it. Cottonwood Lane was on the right. I barely slowed down as I exited from the main road. Lewis Hamilton, the Formula One race car driver, would have been proud the way I took that corner. My car fishtailed in the loose gravel, but I handled the wheel with a smooth action, spinning it the opposite direction to straighten her out, then pounded the gas again. My cabin quickly came into sight.

I grabbed my gear and food, headed inside, slammed and locked the door, then drew the shades and sat on the couch, hoping my shaking hands would calm themselves. Yet for the entire night, they did not.

As ordered, I got two days of solid rest, and it was only then that I found the courage to open the front door. So far, I had only raised some of the blinds to stare outside at the beautiful autumn day. According to the digital thermometer, it was 63F outside. Just the way I love it. I wanted to go enjoy the weather but forced myself to be patient.

"Rest. Doctor's orders," I said. Then, lifting the blind, I added, "I wonder if the town is still full of monsters?" I went to the table, then the fridge. "I better have enough food for the next four days." Yes, I talk out loud when I am nervous. I always have. You will have to excuse my ramblings. "I'm *not* stopping in that cursed place again unless my life depends on it."

That night, when a knock rattled my door, I nearly jumped out of my skin.

"Who the hell is that?" I eyed the door with valid fear. Except for my trusted house sitter, who was caring for my fur babies in my absence, no one knew where I had gone.

"Who . . . who . . . who is it?" Great, I sounded like a freakin' owl. That should scare any bad guys away, right? I huffed at myself for acting like a frightened toddler. "That's not embarrassing, is it!" I mumbled. The knock came again.

I slunk toward the door. First, I deviated to the nearest window to edge back the blind, then flicked on the porch light. My eyes shot wide. "Hot damn!" The most beautiful woman I had ever laid eyes on stood waiting. And, as a friggin' bonus, she wasn't a monster. I unbolted the locks, grabbed the doorknob and twisted, then flung the solid piece of wood open.

She bore a Celtic look. Pale skin with long, flowing red hair pulled back into a ponytail. Emerald green eyes stared into mine. Her toothy white smile was perfectly straight and nearly blinded me. She had an athlete's body, firm and proud. She looked flawless.

"Hi there. I'm horn . . . I . . . I . . . I mean, I'm Orin." You blithering idiot! That was a great first impression.

She smiled and extended a hand. "I'm Amanda." We shook before she went on. "My family owns this place, and I came to be sure you're satisfied. Do you have everything you need?"

My mind went to places it shouldn't have. I certainly couldn't say what I was thinking. To hide my reddening face, I stepped back and swept my hand inside.

"Come in. See for yourself. Everything is perfect. And you just add to the place's beauty."

"Awww, that's sweet," she said as she passed, bringing the scent of wildflowers with her. As nonchalantly as I could manage, I inhaled her fragrance. Absolutely glorious.

"Are you alone?" she asked as she turned round.

Hold the phone! Is she wanting to know because she already senses my irresistible charm? Internally, I laughed at my own joke. Actually, I wasn't joking, but I am not writing about some low-grade smut movie. She didn't come here to bed me. Drats!

"It's just me," I replied. "Yep. All alone." I was hoping she would have sympathy. Maybe we could make a connection that way. I know, my actions are despicable.

I motioned to the small living room and began my story as she settled into the only recliner. Naturally, I left out the parts about the townsfolk being creatures from a dark realm or some undiscovered distant outer-rim planet. That shit only happens in movies, not real life.

It's my concussion, I told myself. That's how I imagined it all. It was a viable explanation I could live with. But what if I'm wrong? Maybe I am the only one who can see these beasts *because* of my condition. Oh, snap! Why did I have to go and ruin perfectly acceptable reasoning by throwing logic into the ring?

As I neared the end for the reason of my visit, my gorgeous guest leaned forward, seeming unusually interested in my dry-as-paint story. Her toothy grin spread wide. And for an instant, only an instant, I thought those pearly whites had grown fangs. I rubbed my face and looked again. Nothing. She was as beautiful as ever and still smoking hot. That made things much easier to explain away.

"There are some great places to eat in town," she offered. "Want to go to dinner?"

Jackpot! Did she just ask me out? What *is* happening? Things like this never happen to me. Is this all a part of my imagination? My fantasy after having been locked away for two days?

Torn between panic of stepping back into Creature Town and boyish excitement of possibly getting lucky, I had no idea what to say. My emotions rode the roller-coaster express. Hell yes, I wanted to spend time with her. In my mind, I was dancing like M.C. Hammer singing, *Can't Touch This*. Stop! Hammer time!

This cursed trip may be worth it after all. Then the brakes came on to ruin everything. I switched into full fear mode. What if Sasquatch or the werewolf returned? What if someone else got gruesomely murdered before my eyes again? Don't get me wrong, I love horror movies, just not ones I am trapped in. The idea of being a monster's snack is sort of a turnoff. It's hard to get certain body parts working when you're worried about being murdered at every turn, if you get my drift.

But as I gazed back into her bright, alluring eyes, I decided to jump at the chance. Danger be damned. I'm going into Indiana Jones adventure mode. "I'd love to go."

She perked up. "Great! You drive."

My stomach churned during our short trip. I was nervous over our date, if that's what it was, and at crossing paths with Black Lagoon dude, Sasquatch, or worse. I just wanted a normal evening with a stunningly beautiful woman who did not come off as freakish or a twisted creature feature star.

She pointed to a cozy-looking restaurant just off the main drag. It looked clean and well kept. At least on the outside. Though, I did laugh at the name. The Dew Drop Inn. Really! That's the best they could come up with? What about The

Monster Menagerie or Travelers are Tasty? This *is* Hicksville, I mused. Though, due in part to the stunning woman by my side, I refrained from saying anything.

Inside, we slid into a darkened corner booth, received great service from a waitress that looked wonderfully normal, then began to chat as we waited. The more she talked, the faster I knew I could fall for her. Amanda fascinated me with amazing stories from all over the world. She had seen and done things I have only dreamed about. I wondered if she was making them up to impress me, but the primal part of me—which was growing stronger by the second—simply refused to care.

She excused herself to the ladies' room. Perfect. I needed to check in with my house sitter. It had been long enough. A few quick texts wouldn't hurt, right? I freed my phone and grimaced as the bright screen shined in my eyes. It hurt more than expected.

I squinted and tapped on the keyboard for a few moments, then hit send. My critter-nanny responded instantly. My fur babies were fine and that made me happy, but I was being stupid. I rushed the texting thing. It really hurt. I sat rubbing my temples as our waitress returned.

She poured me some more water as I stowed my phone. As I glanced up to say thank you, panic returned. Six spindly black legs stretched forward; two beady black eyes watched me. She's an insect! I gripped the table as a bolt of dread ripped through me. An ant! Our waitress is a five-foot-tall freakin' ant! I tore my stare away and peered straight ahead, hoping Amanda would return soon.

Why! Why am I seeing this? And for shit's sake, why now! Is this place cursed? Just as things are starting to go great with a wonderful woman, I see monsters again.

Our waitress's legs reached out, taking my coffee cup next, and filled it. I had to be sure, I thought. I need another peek.

Putting on a fake smile, I flicked a quick glance. Yep, she's an insect. My relentless table grip tightened.

"Can I bring you anything else?" she asked.

I wanted to ask for a giant can of bug spray but shook my head instead. "N . . . n . . . no, thank you."

I breathed a sigh of relief as Amanda returned to ease into her seat. She stared at with me concern, resting her hand on mine. My loins stirred a bit. Her touch was soft, and she smelled so good. "Are you okay, Orin?"

Our eyes met. Oddly, she looked different, too, but I couldn't put my finger on it. She didn't have claws, and no horns were growing out of her head. Not that I had seen any creatures like that yet, but what the hell, why not dream big. Maybe Godzilla is around, too.

"I'm fine. Thank you for asking."

I surveyed the restaurant as coolly as possible, but with every moment my composure slipped further. There were no murders to witness, yet now I was surrounded by monsters and creatures of every kind again. They had all appeared normal when we entered. Why did they change? Maybe I need a shrink more than a doctor. Maybe I have some undiscovered mental disease. Maybe my life was destined to make me a test dummy for a new affliction.

Dinner turned horrible. I could barely concentrate on Amanda's voice. I heard no more of her stories. The clicking of pincers, low growls, buzzing, throaty roars, and more drowned out my every thought. It was a constant, unrelenting nightmare. I decided to leave my 'vacation' tomorrow. Unless, of course, the possibility of great sex tonight was on the table. Then I would be convinced to stay one extra day. But I'm not leaving the cabin again until my time is up.

But if she decides to go home tonight, I am packing and hitting the road once the sun rises. I would leave tonight but am smart enough to know I need rest first. I can't drive four hours in this shape but there must be a bus, cab, or Uber somewhere nearby.

Finally, the meal was over. I paid without ever making eye contact with Ms. Pincers, our ant—I mean, waitress. During our exit I saw an octopus woman, a werewolf couple, more Lagoon creatures, and some things I have no idea what the hell they were. Earthlings have nothing to compare them to. Ugh!

Pulling the phone from my back pocket, I squinted at the screen to text Doc Marsden. Another violation, I know. But I had to let her know what I had done and what I now needed. *Need to see you. Help me. My headaches have grown worse. Things are so weird right now.*

Amanda weaved her arm into mine as we headed for the car. We looked like a young royal couple taking a casual stroll in the night. Though, she felt a bit cold. I took off my zip-up sweatshirt to wrap it round her shoulders.

"Better?" I asked.

She smiled at me and nodded. The fangs were there again, larger and brighter, but I refused to believe anything I saw. I wanted to curl up in a corner and have a good cry. Maybe I'm under too much pressure. Like I said, shrink, not a doctor.

She thanked me as I held her car door open. She slid inside. I closed it and moved toward my driver's door when an awful scream broke the night from up ahead. I froze.

A woman burst out from an alley, running hard and screeching like a banshee as her feet pounded against the pavement. Her clothes were tattered in spots, and her forehead was bleeding, blinding her in one eye as the crimson river flowed freely. Fear was in her good eye, which bulged open like a dinner plate.

I wanted to help but didn't know how. What was she running from? Then I saw it. A King Kong-sized spider skittered over the top of the nearest building to descend onto the street in a blink. It was on her seconds. One long, hairy leg knocked her off her feet, then another held her down. The monstrosity drew close, stepped over her, then jabbed her with a stinger. She went limp as the beast wrapped her in webbing before carrying her off.

I still hadn't moved. There is no doubt, I'm unsure of everything right now.

In a daze, I slid into the car and drove in silence. Thankfully, Amanda reached out to intertwine our fingers. Touching her cold, pale skin broke my trance. She gently traced the veins on the back of my hand.

"You have wonderful veins. They raise up like a healthy, virile man's hand," she said as we came to a stop in the driveway. "I find that sexy."

Fireworks went off in my head, sparkling, multi-colored lights dancing before my eyes as I pictured us doing the horizontal mambo. I know it's a long leap from saying my veins turn her on to us bumping knees during hot sweaty sex, but a guy can dream, yes?

Inside the cabin, she wasted no time. She pulled me to her with surprising strength. If I didn't know better, I'd say she lifted me off the ground and moved me like a chess piece. I tried not to think of it since my blood flow was not solely running to my brain or hands.

Soon, after some fondling and kissing, we were naked in bed—a dream come true. I had never been with a woman so satisfying in all my life. She knew every place to touch, was a sensual kisser, and her body was perfectly firm beneath me, on top, and . . . you get the picture. I was turned on.

Next, once we had both gotten our desires taken care of, I lay staring at the ceiling hoping this feeling would never end. My gorgeous redhead lay next to me, her thigh laying atop my groin as she fingered the vein in my neck. Her touch was beyond exciting. I was getting ready to rise to the occasion again. And so, it seemed, was she.

With an unexpectedly swift move, Amanda straddled my hips, then leaned forward to kiss me, nibbling her way past my ear and down to my neck. Then, the stinging pain made my legs stiffen. My feet twitched, yet I could not move. She held me down like I was a helpless child.

Was I hypnotized? Did she slip something in my coffee earlier? I was paralyzed. Thankfully, the pain subsided in seconds. Then things became hazy. I felt weak. Very weak. I was suddenly tired. Exhausted to the point of numbness. Too much sex, perhaps? No, that can't be it. I can never get enough.

Amanda sat up, her nakedness displacing my fear for a moment as she moved slowly against my groin. She wiped my blood from her fangs and lips.

"My, you are delicious," she said. "I drank a bit more than intended. You have my apologies." She slid off to get dressed as I lay helpless, barely able to form words. "I'll leave you to die now and come back later. I promise. You'll need to be disposed of."

Disposed of! To die! What the hell does any of that mean! Still, no words came. I tried to beg her to save me. To stay. To make me like her. Anything but kill me. I'm too young to die. I wanted to scream out loud but could not.

She bent to kiss me goodbye, then left without looking back. Fighting the weakness as best I could, and with all my fading strength, I pulled myself from bed, crawled to the living room to retrieve a notebook and pen, then began to write what you are reading now.

As I mentioned from the start, I am dying. Short of a seven-pint transfusion, nothing can save me. I think she drained nearly every drop of my blood.

Remember this. Please, always trust your visions. Be afraid of them. They are true. Each one. It is not your imagination.

I hope someone finds this journal. If my words can save just one life, it was worth it.

So weak. So empty. So cold.

I

am

soooo

cold.

Soooo————

Eyes in the Dark

The night pressed in like a suffocating shroud as Eleanor trudged the narrow, uneven path toward Hollowbrook Manor. The mansion stood as a decaying monument to the past, its crumbling walls emerging from the fog like the remains of an ancient, dead beast.

The windows stared out like hollow eyes, their black depths eerily watching her approach. The air carried the scent of rot. Nearing the house, she thought she heard an unnatural voice whispering tales of forgotten tragedies. She shook it away.

Once a proud estate, now it was little more than a mausoleum to the family that had once filled its rooms with life —*a family she had once known.*

Eleanor had never planned to return. Her uncle, Albert, the last elderly Hollowbrook, had passed away weeks ago, leaving her the house in his will. Eleanor's siblings wanted nothing to do with it. They were terrified of the place. Besides, she was the oldest, so the honor—if it could be deemed as such —fell to her. She was officially the heiress of the manor and lands.

It was hers now, all of it—its history, secrets, ghosts, or whatever else lay inside. The thought of stepping inside again, of breathing the same air that had once felt so stifling, made her heart flutter.

Just as she remembered from her youth, the iron gate groaned on its rusted hinges, a sound that pierced the silence and stirred something deep and uneasy within her. Her perfectionist father had oiled and repaired it countless times, muttering about craftsmanship and pride. Yet no matter how meticulously he worked, the gate had always screamed in protest, as though it resisted silence by nature. It had creaked since the day she was born—perhaps long before—and now, after all these years, it still cried out like a thing alive, unwilling to forget.

The manor stood shrouded in shadow at the edge of a dense forest. Its grounds were overrun with creeping ivy and wild brush. Nature, relentless and patient, was reclaiming what had been abandoned, what man had built and left to decay. Eleanor's footsteps crunched along the gravel path, each one unnervingly loud. The sound echoed through the stillness surrounding her, a silence so complete it seemed to wrap itself around her like something alive. *It has always been quiet here. Have I noticed that before?*

As expected, the front door was locked. Aunt Agnes had been a woman of strict routine and careful habits. Eleanor had no doubt the house—now hers—would reflect that same unsettling order, tidy on the surface but hiding whatever rot lay beneath.

Reaching into her coat pocket, she pulled out the heavy iron key. The cold metal bit into her fingers as she fit it into the oversized lock. The door resisted for a moment, then creaked open with a long, low groan. The manor's vast interior stretched out before her, dark, empty, and waiting.

The air still smelled of damp wood and mildew, a scent that pulled memories from the corners of her mind with startling ease. She had spent many nights here as a child, her family gathered around the fireplace while Aunt Agnes or Mildred recounted tales of the Hollowbrook ancestors. Back then, each evening felt like a rich history lesson, filled with pride and reverence for the family name.

But at times there was a sense of dread in the way her aunts spoke of the house, as though something watched them from the shadowed corners of each room or passage. Something sinister, dark, and angry.

Closing the door behind her, Eleanor noticed a great hallway stretching long and narrow, like a creepy corridor to a forgotten tomb. The wallpaper was peeling, the chandeliers sagged, their crystals dusty with age. As she reached the grand staircase, Eleanor paused.

She touched the banister but didn't move. Was it her imagination, or had she seen something out of the corner of her eye? A flicker of movement. Something watching her?

Mere imagination or a cruel trick of light, perhaps reflecting from the medieval suit of armor or Celtic deity statues? Maybe the Aboriginal figurines or the Egyptian divinities, which stood in somber silence as they faced outward, ever watchful.

This place is creeping me out. No wonder I'm jumpy. But I'm sure it's nothing more than my imagination.

It was then a faint voice drifted through the air, like the sound of dry leaves rustling in the wind. She spun quickly, but the hall was empty, save for the shadows.

It was nothing. Nothing. Just imagination. She repeated her earlier words to convince herself. Still, she couldn't shake the feeling of being watched. The knowledge lay bare on her skin,

119

apparent in the raised flesh along her arms and goosebumps covering her legs.

Eleanor made her way through each level of the darkened house, her hesitant footsteps falling softly on the worn carpet. She passed rooms filled with furniture covered in dusty sheets, remnants of days long gone. But as she reached the drawing room, she stopped again.

The thick mahogany door was slightly ajar. Slowly, cautiously, she opened it. The room was cold, colder than the rest of the house. It was dim, lit only by the pale moonlight filtering through the filthy windows. But the cold is not what made her blood run cold. It was the eyes.

There, on the far wall, a portrait hung crookedly. It was an old painting; one she had seen many times before. It was of her great-great-grandfather, Lord Hollowbrook. His dark eyes stared out from beneath a thick brow. But the eyes . . .

They were different this time. Not still, not lifeless. They moved in slow deliberate fashion, tracing her every step with an unnatural awareness. Eleanor gasped. Her skin prickled with fear.

She remembered reading about the Mona Lisa effect—a trick of perspective where a painting's eyes seem to follow you, no matter where you stand. But this was no illusion. These eyes were not painted to appear alive. They *were* alive.

Something behind the oils and canvas watched her. Not with admiration or indifference, but hunger. It was the kind of attention that made the hairs rise on her neck before her mind even caught up. The gaze didn't just shift; it locked onto her with the weight of something old and patient. Something that had waited a long time to be seen again.

No matter how many times she looked away, she always knew exactly where those eyes were. Even with her back turned, she felt them drilling into her, measuring her, inspecting her like an insect under glass.

And then—she swore—they blinked.

Just once, and that was enough. She reeled in terror. This wasn't a painting; it was something wicked. And something inside it had just *stirred from a long slumber.*

Against her every instinct, she stepped closer again, her legs feeling heavy, as if dragging a weight. Her eyes raised.

Hollowbrook's eyes glinted back with a cold, unnatural gleam.

Shadows pressed closer, stretching toward her like unsettling dark hands. Another gasp burst from her lips as Hollowbrook's eyes grew larger, more vivid, their gaze sharpening into something she could not explain. Sinister? Evil? Vile, perhaps?

"Eleanor," said a low voice. Had it come from the depths of the painting itself? It was certainly her name, but not her aunt's voice, not any voice she knew. It was graveled, guttural, and filled with malice. "You should not be here. You should not have come."

Terror jolted through her, sharp and sudden. The repulsive eyes remained unblinking and fixed, never straying from her face. Their gaze gripped like a vice, cold and inescapable, squeezing something from deep within her she did not want to give—her sanity.

In desperation, she turned to flee. Instead, the door slammed closed. A distinct locking sound filled the room. *Trapped! It can't be!* Blind terror reigned as she struck the door with her fists and feet.

"Let me out! Help me! Help! I want out!"

Voices came next—soft at first, like a faint wind rising in volume while a chorus of voices called her name. She spun, desperate for the source, but only the portrait eyes met her, glowing faintly in the darkness, coming alive with malevolent hunger.

Suddenly, eyes were everywhere. The figurines, statues, and even the portraits were no longer lifeless, no longer still. They all watched from the shadows.

Something darted from behind the chair, a flicker of movement swallowed quickly by the darkness. Shapes shifted along the shelves, slithered across the ceiling, crawled along the floor —silent, formless things unseen in the daylight. Now, they were watching. They had always been watching.

"You cannot leave," said the first voice again. This time it was closer, as though it were standing right behind her. "We have seen you. We will never let you go."

Again, Eleanor reached for the door, her shaking hand gripping the cold knob, twisting and pulling with all her strength. Finally, whether through luck, or some horribly malicious game, the door swung wide. She dashed from the room to bolt down the hall.

Taking the steps two at a time, she raced toward the entrance. Yet the eyes followed, still watching, still hunting.

Lost in dread, Eleanor never realized they had been guiding her all along, appearing just long enough to make her turn, to nudge her down one hallway instead of another. Their subtle presence was deliberate.

She ran through the darkened house, breath shallow, as shadows brushed against her skin. Still, the eyes never blinked, never turned away. Like in the room, they were everywhere—lurking in corners, covering the walls, even hovering above her, silent and patient. Always watching. Patiently waiting.

Finally, a wave of relief washed over her as the front door came into view. Laughter and whispers chimed in as she flung it open with a final scream.

The fog outside was thick, but at least it was not as oppressive as the house. Her car was nowhere to be seen as she ran into the night, the weight of the eyes still pressing on her mind.

As she fled, the dense murkiness parted, and for the briefest moment, she saw the silhouette of the manor standing behind her, as lifeless as it had been before. But the eyes were there, staring from the broken windows, from the trees lining the path, from above and below, from the very darkness of the night itself.

The madness continued as she ran.

They would never let her go.

Phantasm

The blood trail was fresh. The crimson beads lay atop the cobblestones of Oxford Street in an erratic pattern reflecting darkly in the fading moonlight. Alix Strong studied the scene with a critical eye and an extra layer of apprehension.

Her worry was due not to the gruesome sight, but one fashioned from her own desires. She had to prove herself and do it quickly. The weight of her achievement—the first-ever female Detective Chief Inspector, or DCI—did not come lightly; rather, it suffocated her. For months, demonstrating her ability remained her highest priority, yet she currently had little to show for the new title. She hoped finding this perverted serial killer in short order would go a long way to that end.

Thirty yards away lay a victim's dismembered body—the fifth horrible mutilation in as many weeks. Townsfolk were terrified. Most refused to leave their houses. Parents kept children inside. Street prostitutes travelled in bunches for safety. The more affluent women walked in pairs or groups. Men took to openly carrying clubs, knives, or pistols. Meanwhile, the

Detective Chief Inspector grew angrier each day the murderer remained free.

"The killer got careless," noted Alix, pointing to a perfect shoe imprint in a viscous pool of blood. "About a size six, I'd say. Means either man or woman, so it's not much to go on. But it's something."

Her partner, Mortimer—Mort to his colleagues—squatted beside her. "The trail vanished back there. It heads the direction of Regent's Park." He jerked a thumb over her shoulder. "There's not enough left of our victim to tell if she fought back. Did her blood drip off the killer, or did she wound them during the attack, and the blood belongs to our attacker?" he asked softly, thinking out loud more so than asking her opinion. "Bloody hell, we have a mess on our hands. And it's not helping that folks are scared stiff. If they brave outside their homes, they see a killer in every stranger they pass. Folks are losing their minds and attacking innocent people out of their own fear. We must stop it."

"Was it actually a person who did this?" asked Alix, cringing at her words. In her head, the question sounded perfectly logical, but once uttered, it seemed foolish. "It looks like starving animals tore her apart, just like the others. How could anyone have done such a thing and remain unseen?"

Mort frowned and tilted his bowler hat back. "Right you are. Excellent question. Without more to go on we may never know. We're looking a bit incompetent on this. The Detective Chief Superintendent is totally cheesed off that we have no leads." He straightened his hat as they moved back to the corpse.

Alix swept a hand before her. "There is so much hate here. You can feel it. How could anyone do this to another human being?"

"Hold it together, dearie," said Mort. "You knew this job could be unpleasant."

"Mort!" she said firmly while wagging a finger his direction. "I've asked you to stop using those words on me. I am not your sweetie, dearie, honey, or any other such thing. Alix, partner, or DCI Strong is fine," she said, her inner strength rising in her tone. "Call me any demeaning name again and you'll be sitting down to have a whiz."

Mort chuckled. "True enough, you have asked." He touched the brim of his hat. "Apologies, partner."

She accepted it with a nod. *That was a small victory, I hope,* she thought.

"By the way, I know working with a woman, especially since this is my case, is hard for you and most men to under-stand, but I am just as good as anyone else on the force. I worked bloody hard to get here and I've earned it. I am the first one who has done every bit of training while graduating top of my class," she added.

Mort nodded agreement. "No doubt, times are changing, and women are rising up. Personally, I have no problem with it, especially since many do a man's job better than some of the slobs I've worked with. But you being the DCS's niece doesn't sit well with some. They think you got here from ridin' his coat-tails. Several more experienced men got passed over for you to take this spot. It has caused a load of bad feelings, no? I don't envy you."

"Well, maybe they should've been better at their positions to move ahead in the world instead of relying on the thing hanging between their legs. That doesn't get it done in my book." She paused as anger swelled in her. She knew full well men talked about her behind her back, yet Mort's truth prickled her skin. "I wanted to partner with you since you're honest with me. I respect that. It's why we work together so well."

"Then let's catch a killer, partner," said Mort, changing the subject.

Around them, the sky lightened to a dull grey as daylight pushed away the night. Alix breathed deeper as darkness fled. Her long-held fear of ghosts or monsters would not come for her now. At least not until the sky darkened again. She extinguished her lantern and handed it to a patrolman before pulling out her notebook and heading for the nearest flat.

Two slow hours passed as the inspectors questioned residents. Many were no help. One nervous man spoke of drifting shadows and vaporous apparitions, but his story was discarded as drunken lunacy. The detective duo left his flat wearing knowing smiles.

Normally, Alix would have taken a strong interest in his story. She held more faith than most in things that lay beyond human understanding, but even she could not look past the man's sloshed state, which had put his credibility firmly in the loo.

"Bit of a loon, that one." Mort brought his fist to his mouth and tilted his head back to make chugging sounds. "On the hard stuff is my guess."

"Agreed." Alix pondered the account. "Or maybe he did see something and in the dark the attacker looked like a shadow. We should talk to him tomorrow after his bevvy wears off."

Mort shrugged. "He's a sot. His drunk may never wear off. Feels like a waste of time." He straightened his coat and scarf. "Did you even get his name?"

Alix patted her ever-present notebook. "Of course. It was Bern Evans." She clucked by pushing her tongue against her teeth several times. "I thought you were a Detective Inspector? You seriously have forgotten a name from two minutes ago."

Mort laughed. "Hold on! It's not that at all. I just hate wasting time on drunks. That bloke was hammered and couldn't find his arse cheeks with both hands. He's too dodgy to be a reliable witness."

———

The torrential rain subsided as the thick clouds broke apart, reducing the moist morning to a chilled drizzle. Horse hooves clacked on the cobblestones as the carriage headed along Portland Place before turning left onto Oxford Street. The cabbie stopped before Bern's flat. The inspectors clambered out.

"Well, at least we're not soaked," said Mort as he shivered. "But the damp creeps into these old bones." He grimaced as he moved his shoulder. "Bit stiff, y' know."

Alix laughed. "You act like you're ninety." She patted his arm in sympathetic fashion. "How old are you? Thirty? Thirty-five, at the most?" She rolled her eyes. "Stop it."

Mort grumbled under his breath. "How did I ever get stuck with you?" He worked the door knocker. "This is a complete waste of time. But this is your case so I am along for the ride . . . no matter how bumpy it may be." He gave a sly wink.

Before Alix could offer a response, Bern answered, looking clean, sober, and chipper. Despite having no recollection of either inspector, he led the pair to the small parlour to offer seats. Alix took a comfortable, overstuffed chair while Mort occupied one end of a purple couch. Bern took the opposite end. The slow-burning fire crackled in the hearth behind them.

Alix freed her notebook and read on, forced to recount the previous night's entire conversation to loosen Bern's memory.

He listened as he moved to the bar and held up an empty glass to offer drinks. Mort and Alix both declined.

"It's nine o'clock in the morning, mate," said Mort. "Who gets leathered that early?"

"Right you are. So y' know, I'm quittin' the drink. After what I saw last night, I want no more to do with being sloshed. Still, I'm feeling right chipper this morning." Bern put the bottle back on the shelf and took a seat.

Alix neatly placed her notebook on her lap and poised her pen over the top of a blank page. "Okay, we're caught up. Now, tell us more about last night. Every detail is helpful, even if you think it's not worth mentioning."

Bern nodded several times. "Y' see, I had the window open a bit, just there." He pointed across the room to a worn recliner facing the street. "I was havin' a ciggie when I heard a commotion. Two people were having a go at one another, pushing and shoving, y' see. A row, right there in the street, mind ya'." He paused as if to gauge the inspectors' reactions.

"Go on," said Mort, simply wanting the story over.

"Well, the lady was tellin' the gent she wanted nothin' to do with him. They were still havin' at it when a shadow drifted past. As sure as I'm sittin' here, it was a ghost. Sunk right into the man's chest, it did. I seen it plain enough by the streetlamp."

Alix worked herself closer to the seat's edge, giving an unseen quiver as the idea of a supernatural killer resurfaced in her mind. "Then?"

"The fella changed into some kinda' monster. Enormous, he was. He started hittin' and slashin' her with these claw-like hands. Tore her to pieces." Bern shuddered. "I nearly lost me dinner right there on the floor." Another point across the room. "Possessed by the devil. I just know it. Worst thing I ever seen."

"What else?" probed Mort, his voice calm with clear disinterest.

"After rippin' her up, he walked away, just like that. Then, I seen the shadow come driftin' out of him to fly away like smoke from a chimney. The gent looked back, and seein' what he had done, went mad and took off runnin' towards Hyde Park. Shrieking into the night. Makin' an awful racket."

Mort leaned closer to sniff the air. "And I'm sure you were a bit pissed when all this happened, no? Drinkin' yourself blind?"

Bern raised a shoulder, looking ashamed. "A bit, guvnor, but I know what I saw." He turned pleading eyes to Alix. "I'm bein' honest. I swear on me mum's grave."

Alix tucked away her pen and notebook, then smiled kindly. "Thank you for the visit. If we need anything else, we'll call again. Cheerio, Bern."

Bern sprang up, looking frazzled. "Y' believe me, right? I swear on me mum's grave that I'm tellin' the truth."

Mort patted his shoulder as he moved past. "Of course, friend. You've been a great help."

Outside, the duo turned left and walked on.

"And now you know why we will never catch this murderin' nut job," said Mort. "Shadows . . . apparitions . . . and chimney smoke. For the love of the gods, he needs to be locked away."

"What if he's spot on?" asked Alix. "Think about it. Not so long ago, humans thought the world was flat. Who decides what is real or imagination? Besides, some things are simply beyond our understanding. Humans don't know everything."

Mort stopped in his tracks, looking shocked. "Not you, too!" He huffed and continued on. "DCI Strong, I put my money on flesh-and-blood killers. Not shadows or ghouls. Think about what you're sayin'. You'll be kicked from the force and locked away if the DCS hears that talk. It won't matter none that you're his niece." He gave her a sideways glance. "And I don't want to break in another partner."

She noticed a hint of budding friendship in his look. "Will you at least keep your mind open to the idea?"

Mort snorted. "To what? Monstrous goblins? Evil fairies or some such thing!" After rubbing his face, he smiled. "Like I said, I'm stickin' with human murderers. Them I can catch while you chase shadows. But I do have one question." He raised his index finger. "Even if you're right, how do you plan on arresting something made of smoke?"

The corners of Alix's mouth turned down. "I'll think of something."

"I have no doubt, partner."

———

Alix once heard of a club named the Society of Psychical Research, or SPR. Several notable, respected men were members, including physicists William Barrett and Lord Rayleigh. Not to mention Arthur Balfour, a rather prominent political figure.

She wondered if these learned men would have some knowledge of possessions or spectres. Could these beings be real or were they simply dredged up from human fears? If the former, it was her hope these men might bear an idea of how to drive it away. She hurriedly arranged an urgent appointment, claiming official police business, which it was, then waited anxiously for night to arrive. Her tremendous fear of ghosts would not keep her from this meeting, she thought. It could not if she wanted to catch this killer and prove her worth.

Alix felt unusually heavy as the carriage rumbled over Westminster Bridge, on to St George's Circus, then swung right, onto London Road. She peered out from the coach window. The rain had fallen away but thick grey clouds remained. There would be no moonlight tonight. *Perfect time for another killing.* She pushed that thought away to concentrate on the passing houses.

Entering the high-class part of the city, or the 'uppity neighbourhood,' as Mort called it, made her nervous. She did not belong here. Normally, she shied away from rich folks, having nothing in common with them, but she needed answers, especially since her own partner doubted her theory. Even she had to admit the concept sounded far-fetched, which only made the trip more essential to her quest.

After arriving at SPR headquarters, Alix was led to a large, ornate sitting room deep within the largest house she had ever stepped foot inside. She nervously lowered onto a settee and waited alone. Around her were finely woven rugs, marbled floors, exquisite paintings, antique statues, and rare books. Finally, she was led to a much smaller room where her hosts sat smoking pipes and drinking expensive brandy and smooth whiskey.

Once talk began, the hours sped by. The amount of information Alix received was staggering. She could barely keep up. It did nothing for her ego to be asking such absurd questions about vaporous beings and paranormal events in the presence of such powerful men, let alone ones deemed as the country's brightest. She felt small and insignificant.

Surprisingly, and to her delight, the three men demonstrated great respect and treated her kindly, never once speaking down to her. However, that remained the only bright spot. Even after hours of attentive listening and nodding, along with several words she would have to look up later to understand their meanings, solid answers evaded her. Her line of

questioning was beyond that of even their esteemed understanding.

After polite goodbyes were said, she was led to the front
door by a well-dressed, attractive servant. The woman tugged
at Alix's sleeve and tilted her head abruptly right. The DCI
followed.

"If I may dare, Miss, my name is Isidora Digby. I am the
Lady's Maid. I heard y' talkin' in there. Every word of it." She
gave a quick look behind her. "I have a habit of listening in
since my Lady asks such things of me. She's just keepin' the
men folks straight, y' understand. Makin' sure they are not up
to no good with other ladies." Another glance over her shoulder, as if being spied on. "Those fellas are smart enough but
don' know about true evil and the like. They try to explain it
away, sayin' evil is because of some scientific reason. They're
wrong. Evil exists because of people. It lies within the heart of
us all at one time or another."

Alix was taken aback by the woman's last words. Was Mort
correct? Was this the doing of a crazed human killer? She held
fast to her own theory. "While that may be true, it does not tell
me what it is or how to stop it. What can I do?"

Isidora took another fleeting glance around. "Yer' dealin'
with an ancient evil whose stories have been told for ages. To
catch it, cause a scene," she said as if the answer was obvious.
"Evil is drawn to anger and hate, y' know. The spirit enters a
person's body to make them do malicious things. After that, it
drives 'em mad or hurries 'em towards their own death."

Adrenaline coursed through Alix's veins like a jolt. Her
description matched the exact scenario Bern described. *This is
it. I'm onto something here.* "Tell me more," she prodded.

"The same thing happened in France before we relocated
here. There were killings like this there, too. People said it was

some lunatic. They never did catch whodunit, because it weren't no human killer, I tell y'."

Alix was stunned. "Do tell," she replied, her voice raising an octave.

"Here's what I know. Get two people carryin' on during the night, in plain sight, and the vile thing will come. They can't help themselves. They thrive on anger. If the folks stand inside a large salt circle, once the spirit enters, it's trapped."

"If it is just a circle, why can't the thing fly out of the top or into the ground?" asked Alix. Once Isidora's face pinched in response, Strong felt her own face souring. This was the third instance in two days she regretted her choice of words.

"Because what looks like a circle to your eyes is really a sphere to the malevolent ones. Have a jar or a vessel handy, one you can seal tight after you trap it. Be sure to put a bit of salt inside first. It binds it there, just like the circle. After catchin' it, take the immoral thing far away and bury it deep. We don' have the power to destroy ancient wickedness, but the container will serve as a prison for as long as it remains unopened. Go place it where no one will ever discover it."

Alix was dizzy with possibilities and hope after the deluge of scholarly information. But she reasoned, as Isidora stood silently with her face mired in shadow, what could she lose by accepting this strange woman's advice? Not to mention Mort already thought her daft, but she could deal with that part. She straightened with resolve as the two shook hands. "Thank you, Isidora. This could save many lives if it works."

"I can help y' Miss. After hearin' your troubles, I went and fetched this." Isidora produced a small purple pouch from within the folds of her dress. She placed it in Alix's open palm. "Keep this talisman close. It guards your soul from being taken over, or worse. I wore it whenever I went out. It helped protect me well enough."

Alix nodded and accepted the gift. "That's very sweet of you. I'll return it after our work is done." She turned to leave only to stop at the door. "If you're wrong, this may be our only meeting."

———

Steady pounding woke Alix from her deep sleep. She sprang from bed, rushing to throw open the front door. Mort stood there, bowler hat in both hands and hair rumpled as if he'd never gone to bed.

"There's been another one," he said as his gaze roved over her. "Hold on! Aren't those the same clothes you had on yesterday? Did you enjoy a few last night?"

Alix blushed, then cursed as she waved a dismissive hand. "Of course not. I don't even drink. Give me a minute. I have a lot to say as we go." She dashed to her bedroom, hurriedly changed into a clean, pressed suit, then grabbed an apple from the counter as she headed for the door.

Mort took in her appearance and shook his head. "I'm never gonna' get used to seeing a woman wearing man's clothing. Looks ridiculous. A bit off, if you ask me."

"Good thing I didn't ask," she replied, bending to pull on her boots. "Besides, I can wear whatever I wish. There's no law sayin' women must wear those cursed dresses and bodices all the time."

"True enough," said Mort as they stepped into the street to hail a cabbie. "I still say it ain't natural, though."

"If you like it so much, you try wearing one of those damnable corsets all day. And high heels, I might add."

Mort fell silent and held the door open for Alix to exit.

"Thank you, fine sir," she said.

Minutes later, in the snug carriage, Alix explained the finer details of her plan, and it wasn't until they had arrived at the bloodied scene that her partner raised his voice.

"Yur' tellin' me we need two fools to risk their lives to catch a ghost? A ghost! Do y' hear yourself? You've gone mad!" He removed his hat to slick back his hair.

Alix grew flustered. "Do you want the killing to end or not? And I never said ghost. You did."

"I think you've been reading a bit too much. This isn't some fictional, chain-rattling story. Blast it all, we need a real murderer, not hocus pocus nonsense with salt and jars."

Discouraged by her partner's refusal to see anything past his own nose, Alix opened the carriage door and trotted out into the cold, overcast morning, moving toward the corpse. The scene was worse than the last. She scowled at the carnage. Jamming a stiff finger toward the body, she said, "This being can't be killed with guns, and science can't solve it. It is beyond us. Look, are you going to help, or shall I do this alone?"

Mort folded both arms across his chest. "I suppose we will be the two fools you're using for bait, no?"

"It's what we get paid all those pounds for," she said as a smile turned the corners of her mouth upward.

Mort snorted. "What if the thing gets in you and you try to kill me? Then what? I am supposed to stick you in a jar? This is pure bonkers."

Alix's mouth fell open. *He's right! What if it gets in me? Would I kill my own partner? Would the talisman work?* These were not questions she desired to answer now, or perhaps ever. Ignoring him and dodging the unseemly answers floating round her mind, she studied the area again.

"Look." She pointed to bloodied footprints. "Like the last time but larger. I bet there's another body here somewhere. If what Isidora said is true, the attacker either went mad or killed themselves. Perhaps both. They likely didn't go far."

Within minutes, as Alix predicated, another body was discovered. The poor woman had plunged a knife into her own throat, then turned the blade sharply. She died still clutching the handle, a pool of fresh blood surrounding her stiffened frame.

Mort lit a cigarette and took a long drag. "Shit! This is total bollocks!"

Alix frowned at him as he exhaled a cloud of smoke. "I thought you quit that disgusting habit."

"I did. Until now," he said. His index finger tapped the top of the cigarette. "Fine, you win. I'll admit your absurd other-worldly idea is seeming more real every second."

"Tonight is the night. Let's draw this thing out and be rid of it once and for all. Either that or wait to be sacked by the Superintendent." Her eyes scanned the growing crowd. "I'm surprised he isn't here by now." She paused long enough to cover the corpse with a large sheet a patrolman handed her.

Within seconds, splotches of soaked-through blood likened the sight to a bizarre abstract painting rather than a murdered body. Alix turned away to face Mort. "Meet me at the station house at dusk. Let's trap this thing and put it far away where it can do no more harm."

Her partner drew a deep breath and slowly let it out. "Providing we don' kill one another first."

———

Alix paced. Her eyes drifted to the clay jar she had bought earlier at a nearby antique shop. It seemed fitting to hold an age-old evil. The latches were stout and the inner walls thick.

Her stomach churned as Mort's difficult questions played in her mind, despite her best effort to ignore them. What if he attacked her? How would she react? She eased her mind by tucking a small cudgel in her coat pocket, just in case. Still, she could not help but fret.

What if Isidora was wrong and the salt would not contain the entity? What if it did not go into the jar willingly? *How does one force a spirit inside a literal everlasting tomb?* The sick feeling grew stronger.

Drawing back the curtains, she stared at the sky. The time had come. Heaving a long sigh, she took up the container and headed outside for a carriage. Her nerves continued, manifesting themselves in rapid bodily motions. The carriage rattled along, her foot joining the rhythm as she tapped the floorboards. Each tap grew louder than the last, blocking all sounds from the outside until she could hear nothing but the roar of her overwhelm. It took every ounce of willpower to suppress the anxious scream lodged in her throat.

Before she realized, Mort climbed into the cab and tipped his hat. "Ready?"

"I have no choice, do I?" It was a rhetorical question. "Did you bring the salt and shovel?"

Mort tapped the shovel handle, then hoisted the ten-pound sack up from his canvas bag. "All set."

Twenty minutes passed before they found a spot near Hyde Park to begin their work. Mort created an enormous salt circle on the ground, effectively enclosing them both. The sight of it calmed Alix's fraying nerves and brought a newfound clarity to her mind.

"Remember the plan and stick to it," she said. "I'll start yelling. You shove me round a bit, then we have an old-fashioned row."

"I hate the idea of layin' hands on you. Just know I don' mean any of it. It's to save lives, y' understand," he said, looking uncomfortable and fidgeting. "Raising a hand to a woman don't sit right with me."

Alix blushed. "Whatever I say I don't mean, either. No matter how angry I seem, it's not personal. Don't forget that."

Mort extended a hand. "No problem at all. Remember, I was married once. I know the drill." They shook on their agreement. "I've got some uniformed fellas nearby. They're to hold back anyone who tries to interfere."

"Great idea. Sharp thinking." Alix pulled her coat tighter from the evening chill, then looked at the open jar by her feet. "It's dark enough. Let's crack on."

Mort started in, yelling several disparaging phrases about women with rude hand gestures to match. His outburst stunned Alix into silence. She was supposed to start. *I'm not as ready as I thought.* Still, her resolve swelled to turn against her partner. Her hand lashed out, striking his cheek with a resounding smack.

Mort's eyes shot wide, surprised by her quick movement. He stepped forward to shove her, but Alix sidestepped and connected a sharp blow to his jaw. His astounded look returned as he lunged forward to seize her arms. More shouting.

Alix grappled with her partner, no longer sure if Mort was acting or not. His face was reddening as though his emotions were boiling over. If he was acting, he was damned good at it.

Then, from their left, the shadow approached like a twisted dream, one which Alix caught from the corner of her eye. It paused to hover behind a thick tree before darting across the open grass field. Swirling and writhing, the entity moved faster than she could conceive. It entered Mort's chest, turning his eyes pure black as he began to shake. Alix released him, staring wordlessly in horror as his body trembled, morphing into a ghastly inhuman shape.

Enormous, clawed hands hung on thick, gnarled limbs. The beast was massive, towering over her as if she was a child. Fanged teeth protruded from its wide, gaping mouth. A rough

139

scaled hide covered its frame. Large feet steadied the beast as it eyed her with a hateful type of bloodlust.

Somewhere in the distance someone screamed at the sight, but she wondered if it was her imagination. Regardless, the beast crouched before her and no help was coming.

Alix quickly backed away as the creature thumped the ground with each step, drawing closer. As if propelled forward, the thing suddenly stood before her, their faces nearly pressed together. Putrid air blew over her face as her attacker swung a limb, barely missing her head.

Quick reactions saved her life. She dived for the jar, but the beast made another rapid move to block her way. She cursed, lunged again, but fell short as searing pain ripped her body. Her leg turned warm as blood flowed into her boot.

She dared a glance, terrified of what she would see. Three deep, linear wounds scored the length of her calf. Incredible pain made her dizzy. She wanted to vomit. Again, the beast stomped forward, shaking the earth as she attempted to crawl away. Agony rooted her after mere inches. She flipped over, both elbows digging into the ground as the beast closed in. Tears of agony blurred her eyes as it pulled back a clawed limb.

With a final surge she rolled from its path, then seized the jar as dirt flew into her face from the strike that shredded the ground. The monster howled in anger and came again as Alix rose to her feet, breathing hard.

"Not used to having anyone fight back, are y'!" she shouted. "Come on! Kill me if you can."

The beast coiled, then flung itself through the air, stretching its large form horizontally. Alix jerked the vessel from behind her back and held it steady, arms shaking against the incoming roar. Unable to stop its momentum, the creature was sucked in, snarling and biting as it clawed the air, trying to gain traction that would not come.

The air spun with cyclonic fury, growing intensely warm as the horror was yanked from Mort's body. Alix gasped for air as the hot wind ripped away her breath. In the moment she grew lightheaded from lack of air, the two—her partner and the entity—separated.

Mort fell away unconscious as Alix slammed the lid shut and clamped the latches tight. Clutching the jar beneath her arm, she limped to her partner's side, gratified to see him rolling over with a groan. Kissing his forehead, she smiled.

"That went well," she said.

Upright now, Mort slowly focused. His eyes found her mangled leg. He pulled off his coat, ripped away a sleeve, and began to wrap her wound while shouting to his hidden men for help. "Come on, you lot! Move your arses!" He patted Alix's hand. "You'll be heading to the doctor's now."

"Like hell I am," Alix snapped, squirming away from him. "I'm going nowhere near a hospital until we bury this thing."

"But—"

"But nothing!" She rose to hop on one leg. Mort placed her arm round his shoulder and supported her weight. "Get me to a coach," she insisted.

Mort hurriedly gathered the officers. "Whisper a word of this to *any* living soul and you lot will be working patrols in the outskirts of the worst little town you can imagine. Not a single, bloody word, mind y'!"

———

Five days had passed since the attack. Mort and Alix returned to the park to sit and stare at the spot where their salt circle had been. Stronger now, Alix walked unaided, but with a limp—one she hoped would go away with time.

"You know, for a woman, you're pretty smart . . . and tough, too." Mort laughed and clapped her back softly.

She punched his arm. "Yur' a proper arsehole!"

"In case I haven't said it, thanks for not letting me die," he added. "I'll partner with you all day long."

"For a man, you're not too bad, either."

————

Decades slowly passed until one day during an archaeology dig on a potentially valuable site, a nondescript little man with suspenders and wire-rimmed glasses unearthed a sealed ornate jar. It held his attention for a long while before he finally freed the vessel from the cold ground.

Deeming it too beautiful to be hidden away, he made plans to display his find in the illustrious British Museum. A thorough, delicate cleaning was all it needed. But afterward, while holding it in his hands to admire it a moment longer, he could not resist seeing what treasures may lay inside.

One day later, unexplained, horrific murders began in his quaint little village.

The Vanishing Woods

The lantern's glow offered little comfort. Its dim orange flame trembled behind the glass, as though each of Hugo's timid steps might snuff it out. If the oil ran dry, he would be alone in the suffocating blackness. The consequences could be dire. He would not have dared enter the woods at this hour if not for his son's missing dog. But the boy was heartbroken without his furry companion, Bruno, and Hugo couldn't bear to see his son so distraught.

The locals called the forest the Vanishing Woods, and for good reason. Few who entered after sunset, man or beast, ever returned. Over the years, fragments had been recovered: scraps of fur, bones, bloodied scraps of cloth, and full limbs. Whatever curse lingered beneath those ancient boughs had taken root long before Hugo was born, and the fear it brought clung to both the forest and the nearby town for generations. Every townsperson was haunted by it, but Hugo had more reason than most to fear it.

His own father had disappeared within these trees, never to be found. Even before that, Hugo's grandfather had been discovered dead in the same forest, his body intact but his head missing. Hugo had been just a boy then, but the image had never left him. To this day, he still visited the grave, laying flowers by the marker, but only in daylight. Somehow, the sun felt like the only thing that kept the forest's deathly grip at bay.

Yet tonight, alone in the suffocating darkness and clinging to the false safety of his lantern, every owl's cry, rustle of leaves, or glint of eyes in the shadows filled him with dread. The sounds and shifting shapes he had earlier dismissed as tricks of the mind—or perhaps his lost dog snuffling through the undergrowth—could no longer be explained away.

Wiping the sweat from his brow, he whispered a silent prayer for protection to the old gods and pressed forward, calling softly into the darkness, "Bruno. Here, boy."

What would Father say, facing such horrendous fear? Hugo pondered the question the farther he ventured. After all, his father had grown up with the same threat. Would he have stood his ground, braving whatever horrors the woods held, or would he have run, as Hugo was so tempted to do this very night?

More noises brought him back to reality. After several nervous glances over his shoulder, he confirmed his suspicion. He was not alone. Some *one*, or some *thing*, followed. If it was Bruno, could a simple whistle bring his faithful friend to him? Hugo's lips pursed, but no sound came. *Perhaps silence is best, for if it's not Bruno, I'll give away my position.*

Pushing forward, his long legs stumbled over the dense forest undergrowth. As his eyes adjusted to the dark, they locked onto a large thicket ahead. *There! Something moved.* He squinted harder, raising a hand as if to block the light, though it was his own mounting dread he sought to shield himself from.

More strange sounds came from his left. Spinning, he caught a fleeting glimpse of a massive, shadowy figure slipping through the trees. *The Mauler!*

144

Childhood tales of the enormous wolf-like beast flooded him. Regardless of the absurd, fairytale-like name, he was convinced the creature was real, as was each awful story he had ever heard. Even to this day, the mere thought of a beastly encounter made him go weak. And now, caught in the beast's home, it spurred him to flee.

As the shuffling quickened, either imagination or reality brought the monster to life as the wavering shadow followed. Hugo swallowed hard and wondered if he could trust his eyes in the blackened recesses of this evil place. Though it mattered not what his mind tried to tell him, his body believed. He pushed himself as fast as he dared without letting the flame flutter and die behind the safety of the glass.

Moonlight from the first-quarter moon spilled over the forest floor as the clouds slowly drifted apart. A flicker of hope stirred. Perhaps he might reach his village alive. But any optimism was short-lived as thick clouds swallowed the pale light, and with it, his fragile sense of safety.

Only the rapid drumming of his own footsteps and the relentless rustling of pursuit filled his ears. The forest seemed alive with haunting echoes: snapping branches, quivering leaves, the hollow thud of something heavy striking a log— sounds that clung to him like evening shadows.

The beast was closing in. Hugo quickened his pace. *Is it toying with me? Playing a sick game of chase with one inevitable outcome—my death? Why not end it now? Why does the beast wait?* He had no answers.

Suddenly, a haunting howl ripped through the night. It came from ahead, too low and dangerous to be Bruno. The large man clamped a meaty hand over his mouth to stifle the scream rising in his throat. Despite knowing the village was near, it felt miles away. Realization took hold as his boots struck the familiar cart path, and again the unanswerable questions rose. *Why run? The beast will catch me easily. Why is it letting me live?*

Legends told of the monster's incredible speed. It was an undetectable blur of dark fur, jagged teeth, claws like razors, and glowing red eyes that pierced straight to your soul. Worse still, if those eyes met yours, you were paralyzed by a terror so deep it stilled your body and mind.

Hugo's eyes narrowed instinctively as the rustling grew louder, closer, nearly on top of him.

With a flurry of motion, bursting from the bushes—nearly causing Hugo to shriek in terror—came Bruno. The German shepherd charged by, barking hardily as he bolted down the trail.

Hugo quickly realized the strange noises continued even after his pet had passed. He ran after the dog. And in that fleeting moment when hope seemed lost, he rounded a bend to see the warm glow of lanterns and flickering torch flames and heard distant voices riding the night breeze. Another hundred yards, and he would be among safety in numbers.

"Look! Over there!" a voice called. "Someone's coming! Hugo!"

With a surge of renewed energy, Hugo sprinted forward, his lantern swinging wildly in his grip. Thirsty, exhausted, and terror-stricken, he stumbled into the square, collapsing onto all fours. His lantern shattered as it tumbled from his hand.

The crowd closed in quickly, their voices a flurry of muffled, bothersome questions he could not make out. Frightened and exhausted, he could focus only on gasping for air.

Two large men hoisted him up, their grip firm as they carried him to a nearby bench and gently lowered him onto the hard wood. A woolen blanket was draped over his shoulders, and a bucket with a ladle was placed before him. Shaken, Hugo nodded in thanks, but his shattered nerves betrayed him as the ladle slipped from his hands, clattering to the ground with a sharp metallic ring. He didn't bother to retrieve it.

Then, soft hands enfolded his, steadying them. He looked up to see Clara standing before him, her smile brave yet shadowed by worry in her eyes.

There was a grumbling around him as the crowd parted. The town mayor, Adolf, forced his way through the onlookers. He was a large man by any measure, and there was no love lost between him and Hugo. The latter had long seen Adolf as little more than a troublesome tyrant—someone who reveled in his power, exploiting it for favors or taking them by force, knowing no one could oppose him.

At the sight of the mayor, Hugo's mind flashed to the countless bodies found in the woods over the years. They had been victims of the beast, yes, but also of Adolf's cruelty. Many had been coerced into hunting the monster by the mayor himself, a fact still weighing heavily on the villagers' hearts.

Adolf stopped, placing his hands on his hips with an air of smug superiority. He stood for a moment, taking in Hugo's state, then crossed his thick arms over his barrel-like chest. His voice boomed, low and mocking.

"Did you try to kill the beast? Or did you run for your life so fast the thing could not catch you?" He laughed a deep sound. "Did you even see the monster?"

Dejected, Hugo lowered his head as the crowd murmurs buzzed around him. "I saw nothing. Only glimpses as it moved through the trees. The howling was horrible."

"Yes! We heard it, too!" boomed Franz, the blacksmith, his massive frame a mirror of his thunderous voice. "The noise woke us all. That's why we're here—to protect the village in case the beast comes hunting tonight."

"I saw it through the trees!" cried Gustav, pointing toward the woods. "It was eight feet tall, if it was an inch!" His eyes flicked nervously to the dark forest. "Its eyes blazed with red fire."

"Silence!" Adolf's command cut the air like a whip. His eyes narrowed on Hugo, full of disdain. "What say you, coward? Why did you—"

"Shut your mouth, you pig!" Clara's voice rang out, sharp and fierce, as she stepped before Hugo like a shield. The crowd fell into stunned silence. Only the hoots of owls and the crackling of torches was heard. "If you're so fearless, go hunt the monster yourself!" She spat at his feet. "Go on! Take your precious gun and hunt the thing alone. Do what others have failed to do for ages!"

Low whispers rippled through the crowd like a wave, quickly encircling the bickering trio.

Glenda, the blacksmith's wife, stepped forward to grab Clara's hand in solidarity. "She's right. Go on, swine! You've been sending our men into the woods to die while you sit on your fat backside and bark orders just because you're mayor. Well, no more!"

The crowd's buzzing grew louder, spreading like wildfire, and the air hummed with rising defiance. Adolf stepped away, his features briefly faltering in shock before twisting in fury.

"I run this town! The laws are mine to make! I—"

His words halted as a series of sharp barks and a long, wailing howl echoed around them. The crowd fell deathly silent. Instinctively, their eyes turned to Adolf.

"Form a circle! All able-bodied men, to the street!" he commanded. The men sprang into action; several grabbed short swords or axes, their weapons a poor match for the beast lurking nearby. Some clutched small pistols, though they looked hardly more than toys in the face of such danger. Others, paralyzed with fear, scattered to hide—ducking beneath wagons, wedging themselves into any empty space they could find.

Adolf grabbed his belt, hoisting his pants up with a sharp tug. "The time is now! Follow me! The monster is close. We can end this tonight. I'll show you how to kill this cursed thing!"

Hugo spoke softly when the mayor's bravado finally faded. "He's right. We have lived in fear for too long. It's time we stand and fight." He turned to Clara, his expression hardened. "Load the wagon. Take Hans, Frieda, and our pets to your Mutter and Vater's house. They'll take care of you. If I don't return, never come back here. Not for any reason." He took her hand, squeezing it firmly. "Swear an unbreakable vow. Promise me."

Clara's eyes welled with tears. "Ich verspreche." She lowered her head, then repeated her words in English, her voice breaking. "I promise."

Satisfied, Hugo pulled her close for a lingering hug, his fingers gently stroking her hair. "Go now," he whispered.

With a final kiss to her forehead, he turned away. Grabbing a double-headed axe from the pile of weapons, its weight grounding him for a moment, he strode into the woods. Behind him, a small group of men, led by Adolf, followed in grim silence until they reached the forest's edge. They stopped, again waiting for orders.

Adolf pointed ahead, his voice sharp and commanding. "Franz, Gustav, and I will take the left. Hugo, Maximillian, and Otto, you go right. Form a tightening circle until the thing is surrounded. Then we end this. Do not let it escape!" His eyes swept over the men as a scowl twisted his face. "Be quick, you fools! We will only get one chance."

"But the monster moves faster," said Otto, the town doctor

and Hugo's best friend. "We have no chance against it. It will kill us all."

Adolf snorted as he grabbed the doctor's tunic, pulling him close. "Do as you're told, or the town will call in your loan note. How will you survive with no home, doctor?" The mayor shoved him away with a frustrated grunt. "Stille, dolt!" His words demanded silence. His eyes went to Hugo. "Do not run this time, coward," he sneered before leading his companions into the shadows.

Around them, the first light of dawn bled into the sky, the gray of morning spreading like a slow wave. Hugo smiled thinly, appreciating the clarity of his surroundings without torches or lanterns. *An easier way to fight. Or a quicker way to die. But if my sight has improved, so too will the beast's vision.*

Barely thirty steps passed under his feet before a bloodcurdling scream shattered the eerie silence, tearing through the stillness with awful clarity. Maximillian turned a sickly shade of pale while Otto trembled in his boots.

Startled by the sound, Hugo glanced at his friends with compassion and understanding but knew they couldn't stay.

Sprinting toward the sound with his partners in tow, he skidded to a stop to stare into Gustav's lifeless eyes. He had been torn in half. His lower extremities, along with a snail-like trail of entrails, lay some twenty paces from his head and torso. One severed arm sat tilted against a tree trunk as if posed in a bizarre, farewell death wave.

Otto retched, the sound coming ragged and harsh. Maximillian stood motionless, his face drained of color. Hugo felt cold acceptance settle over him. *I will not survive this day. Men, no matter how brave, are no match for the monster's cunning and speed.*

His only hope was that his family would escape to Augsburg. It was far, over one hundred thirty kilometers away, but the city was vast enough to protect them from the creature's wrath. *A city that size could defend itself if the beast ever left the forest to hunt for fresh prey.*

Another scream came, sharp and heart-stopping. High-pitched cries followed. Hugo sprinted forward, the growls and barks from ahead growing louder.

Would he finally face the monster? *Can I stand my ground?* He pushed himself harder as he leapt over deadfalls and tore through thorny underbrush that raked his exposed flesh, leaving streaks of blood in their wake.

He came upon Franz, who sat leaning against a thick tree trunk, his bowels resting upon his thighs. Hugo knelt by his side and took his hand as Otto and Maximillian remained frozen behind him.

The blacksmith coughed up blood. "Save yourselves. Run. Now!" His head tilted back as his unblinking eyes moved skyward, forming an endless death stare.

Hugo gently closed his friend's eyelids as a tear rolled down his cheek. "You were a good, selfless man. May the gods guide you to your ancestors."

The frantic sound of Maximillian's footsteps grew distant as he turned to race toward the village. His terror was unmistakable. Then, in a surreal blur, the enormous beast rushed past, swiping at the bolting man's head, sending it flying from sight to land with a sickening thump.

"Max!" cried Hugo. Without another word, he waved Otto to his side, then turned to vanish into the trees, blending into the shadows like wraiths. They traveled some distance before Hugo pointed to a rock crevice. Otto swallowed hard, staring at the narrow opening.

"You hide here. I will come back for you. I promise." Hugo lay a hand on Otto's shoulder. "I give you my word. I will lead the beast away and hope to survive."

"You will be killed." Otto's voice was matter-of-fact.

"It is the only way. At least one of us must survive to tell the tale."

Leaving his friend to squeeze inside, Hugo pushed through shrubs and dense undergrowth, his unease growing with every step. He had done all he could to conceal his friend, but doubt —and the creeping sense of being watched—clung to him like mist rising from the forest floor. Deep down, he knew the creature could smell fear, and his pounding heart betrayed him like beating a bass drum.

The forest seemed alive with the sounds of creaking trees, rustling leaves, distant animal calls, and yet it was all swept away by the overwhelming sense of danger.

A low growl rumbled in the distance. Then, in a sudden flash of motion, a shadow flitted between the trees—a shape too large, too unnerving to belong to any ordinary animal. Hugo wished to run but he could not leave Otto behind.

He crept forward, calculating every step. But the deeper he ventured the more the silence closed in. The world had gone from a dull quiet to a vibrant, pulsating reality. Every detail was sharp, every movement crisp.

His breath came in shallow, controlled pulls as he steadied himself. He felt like an animal—alive, alert, attuned to the very pulse of the world around him.

The resonant growl from earlier echoed again, but it was different this time. It was clearer, more pronounced, as though it were a part of him. Hugo tried to make sense of it all. Was it the creature's presence? Or something else? Something within him?

A voice—his own, distant and yet unmistakable—whispered in his mind. *You are not alone.*

Hugo shifted onto the balls of his feet, ready to spring into motion. His eyes darted, watching the brush and trees, trying to glimpse the creature before it caught him.

Seconds passed before chaos erupted. Shadows moved impossibly fast. A blur of black fur and sinew with eyes gleaming like molten gold in the darkness came near. The creature was no longer just a presence or shadow; it was a force, a physical thing, a nightmare made flesh.

Its body was impossibly large, hunched low, with rippling muscles beneath its mottled fur. Long legs tipped with claws scraped the ground as it stalked forward. Its face was a monstrous blend of canine and something else. Its teeth shone in the faint light, sharp as daggers, and its breath came in steady heaves.

For a moment, Hugo could only stare, frozen in both awe and fear. But then, the world shifted again. His senses heightened further as something deep within him clicked. The creature wasn't just hunting him—it was drawn to him. *How? Why?*

In the blink of an eye, as his revelation dissolved, the beast inexplicably turned and fled. Yet the clarity of the creature's mind—the sorrow, loneliness, and desperation—remained. Hugo was desperate to retain the connection, but it was gone.

A crashing of a different sort filled the air as Adolf came stomping forward. The hatred in his eyes was unmistakable. The fat man's animalistic rage mirrored the very thing Hugo had just felt from the creature, the same intensity, the same drive. The veins in Adolf's neck pulsed with fury as he glared down.

"You!" cried the mayor, his voice low and guttural. "You betrayed us. Left us to die." He lunged forward, wrapping his fingers around Hugo's shirt collar and shaking him.

"Adolf, stop!" Hugo pleaded. "You don't understand. I'm trying to—"

"You're trying to what?" interrupted the mayor.

Mark K. McClain

"Adolf, please . . ." His voice softened. "Rage is not the answer. The creature is just like us. I believe it is a prisoner. Just like you are trapped within the need for constant anger."

Adolf's lip curled in disgust. "Stop talking. You're not making any sense. Idiot!"

Hugo relented, knowing Adolf would not back down. He was too prideful. Violence was inevitable now—whether against the beast or between themselves.

"How did you let this happen, fool!" Adolf pointed toward Maximillian's headless corpse. "Your cowardice killed him! You'll hang for this!"

Anger unlike any he had ever experienced swelled in Hugo's heart. Only an idiot of a mayor would choose now—with the Mauler upon them and three of their neighbors murdered—to fight amongst themselves.

Preparing to fight, Hugo tightened a fist, but it was not to be as a blur passed to carry Adolf away like a child's toy.

His shrieking pleas died quickly as the beast zipped past, leaving only the mayor's pair of worn boots.

After a hurried search for his axe, Hugo pursued. Seconds passed before the great snap of a breaking branch halted him. The smell of blood reached his nostrils. The woods were silent again as he crept into a small, tree-lined clearing.

Adolf was there, his limbs ripped away, his torso impaled on a large broken branch several feet up a gnarled trunk. His head faced rearward.

Hugo teetered on the verge of madness, then hopelessness. He looked away and fell to his knees, dropping his blade by his side.

"Here I am," he cried, pounding his chest. "Finish this! I know there is no escape. Come, have at me. I am unarmed."

He smelled the beast before it came into view. Daring to

154

raise his eyes, Hugo stared at the enormous monster standing mere feet away.

Blood dripped from its claws and muzzle, its lips curled in a snarl, yet sadness lay heavy in its eyes, which were not blazing red as tales told. Its heavy breath landed on Hugo's skin and as their eyes met, Hugo saw not just hunger, but something mirroring his own emotions. Pain. Loss. A longing that transcended the boundaries of species.

Then he knew, the Mauler wasn't simply hunting food, it was hunting something deeper, something Hugo could not quite grasp.

The beast growled, this time quieter, more resigned, as if it had read its prey's thoughts and was responding. Its lips quivered, the primal instinct to strike held in check.

"Why?" Hugo finally asked, his voice a whisper, as though speaking too loudly might destroy the fragile understanding between them. "Why spare me? After all you've done to the others, why me?"

The monster made a whining sound, an agonized echo of something far beyond hunger or fury.

This is more than survival. It was then the puzzle pieces slowly clicked into place. This creature wasn't a mindless monster—it was trapped, driven by something older than any human.

The beast's eyes flickered with an understanding. It waited, like it knew Hugo was on the cusp of an epiphany.

Hugo's mind raced, and then the familiarity hit him. It was not just a connection between hunter and prey, nor was it just a shared survival instinct. The beast's form, its mannerisms, even the way it communicated—were clear human emotions. There was something raw and untamed about its presence.

Could it be? A flash of a memory danced at the edges of his mind—his father, the old stories whispered around the hearth, the legends of an ancient bloodline cursed to walk the earth in monstrous form. Could the Mauler be one of them?

"Are you one of us?" he asked, his voice barely above a breath.

The Mauler stiffened, its body tensing as though struck by the words themselves. The air grew heavier as the forest itself awaited an answer.

For a long moment, neither moved.

The connection returned, flooding Hugo's mind. He saw flashes of the beast's past: a life once lived, now twisted and lost. The pain of the creature's existence. There were immeasurable losses, loneliness, and rage, all of which suddenly felt more real than his own.

Hugo shook his head. "What . . . what are you?"

The beast's lips parted in a grimace, then uttered a sigh. A sigh that spoke of torment, of a curse stretched over ages of time. Hugo felt the weariness in his bones, the ache that stretched across his muscles. But then, the rumbling started again—the beast was transforming.

In a mere instant, Hugo's father stood before him.

Wilhelm's eyes, human but still holding centuries-old sorrow, softened. His face sagged from years of suffering, his body worn with cares from bearing the curse upon his shoulders, but his gaze remained filled with the intelligence and love Hugo remembered.

"I never wanted this," Wilhelm whispered, his voice cracking. "I never wanted to burden you with this curse. But it is our blood, Hugo. Our flesh. It binds us in ways you cannot understand."

Hugo's mind spiraled. His father was the Mauler and now he stood before him like a broken man. A begging, suffering man.

"You must slay me," Wilhelm said, his voice calm and deliberate. "Save me from the eternal damnation I suffer from the gods."

"Never, Father." Hugo glanced at the axe in his hand. The weight of it was much heavier now, symbolic of everything that had happened and everything that could come next. *Slay me.* The words echoed in his mind. How could he? How could he kill the very man who had once been the center of his world? The one who had given him life.

The thought of raising a blade against his father felt surreal, a dream. But the harder truth gnawed at him—the curse lived in their bloodline. Meaning, his children would suffer, too.

His father's voice, quiet and pained, broke through his thoughts. "There are ways to fight it. There are always ways, my son. But none of them are without sacrifice. None are easy."

"Tell me," Hugo said, his voice strained. "Tell me what I should do."

"The curse is bound to our line. To our very essence. I should have died years ago, but the curse has kept me alive. We can never escape it without . . ." He paused, as if searching for some sign of hope. "There is only one way. Only one of us can survive this. But know you cannot rid the family of this curse. I am sorry, my son."

Hugo thought of Frieda and Hans growing up with the same terror he now suffered. He could not bear it.

"My misery has gone on long enough," said Wilhelm, nodding slowly as if he knew the images tormenting his son. "It's the only way, Hugo. I beg you." His father's cold words rang in his ears.

Hugo's mind screamed to run, to find another way, but deep down, he knew there was no escape from destiny.

"Do it," Wilhelm said softly. "You must, if you wish to save me."

The wind blew through the trees again, the silence

stretching between them. Hugo was torn between love and duty; between his father and the monstrous legacy he would soon carry. The question was no longer whether he could do it, but whether he could live with the choice.

"Death is the only release." Their eyes met again. "You must kill me this very day. End my eternal suffering from this existence. I beg you, mein sohn."

Hugo pressed his lips together to stop from weeping. The man before him was but a shadow of his previous self—broken, cursed, and twisted by forces beyond his control.

"Vater," Hugo choked, his voice raw. "How can you ask me to end your life? You're my father. You taught me how to survive, how to fight . . . to be strong. I cannot do this."

Wilhelm stared back with a deep sadness. His lips parted, but the words didn't come, as if he was wrestling with something far darker than his son could understand. Slowly, he shook his head.

"I understand your pain. But I am a prisoner, and so are you, even though you cannot see it yet. You will feel its pull... its hunger... the moment it sinks into your blood. When it does, you will have to make the same choice. The same choice I had to make. The same choice your grandfather made."

Hugo sank further with every word his father spoke. His grandfather. Was this the reason they had found his headless body? It was too much to comprehend.

No! I won't be like you! I won't follow the path of destruction. How could you kill my grandfather? Your own father! He rose shakily, pushing back against the torrent of emotion threatening to swallow him whole. His fists clenched, and for a moment, he thought about throwing the axe into the forest's depths and walking away. But that would not save his children, nor himself. It would not end this nightmare.

"I won't let this curse pass on to my children." Hugo

shouted, his voice cracking with frustration and grief. His eyes filled with tears, but he refused to let them fall. "I won't!"

"I wish I could have spared you," Wilhelm added quietly. "But we are bound by blood. It won't simply vanish because you wish it. It will claim you and your children, too."

Hugo tensed in denial, but knew the curse had already marked him, whether he wanted to acknowledge it or not. It had always been inside him.

"No . . ." he whispered again, this time with less conviction. "I won't lose them. I will not be like you. There must be another way."

Wilhelm's hand reached out, gripping his son's shoulder with a finality that felt like a promise. "I have killed men beyond count, but not from desire. Self-preservation made me do horrible things. Except for Adolf." He nodded toward the remnants of the man. "He killed your grandmother. Years ago, that pig wanted our land. When Oma refused to sell, Adolf killed her in cold blood but never gained the land deed. I have waited for years to settle the score. Though, until today, he refused to step foot in the woods. His way of being brave was to sacrifice others in his stead."

Hugo looked at the axe. "I . . ."

"Someday you will understand and ask mercy from your own children. Your only desire will be freedom from this twisted life. One stroke and it will be done. Quick and painless. Release me." Sadness returned to his eyes. "Pity this old man and do what needs done. You are stronger than you know."

Hugo eyed the blade, then his father, then back again. This curse would disallow him from ever holding his children again or seeing their smiling faces. The opportunity to see them grow was gone. And what of Clara? Someday, she would believe him dead and go on with life. She was strong that way.

Not bothering to hide his tears, Hugo wept again. Wilhelm smiled and hugged him close.

"I am so sorry," he said. "Never forget I have always loved you."

Through tears, Hugo found his resolve. Stepping back, he gripped the handle until his knuckles whitened under the strain. "Forgive me, Vater," he said as the blade whistled through the air in a horizontal stroke. Wilhelm's head dropped to the forest floor to land at his son's feet. The headless corpse tipped backward, kicking up leaves upon impact.

Hugo looked away, but as the seconds passed, he found courage to face what he had done. In death, the old man's lips wore the hint of a relieved smile.

Finally, with remorse guiding him, Hugo made a circular ring of stones, littered it with small kindling, then placed his father's remains inside and struck flint to steel. The pyre was a release of sorts, but the mantle of the beast had been passed. The Mauler would live on in both him and his children.

The dilemma tore his mind into twisted, fragmented thoughts. Despite notions to see his family again, he wondered how, knowing someday he would ask his own children to murder him. That thought alone made his blood run cold.

When the time came, would they see what he had become and take pity and hasten his death as he had just done? Or would they flee in terror knowing their father was the Mauler?

As the black, swirling smoke rose high into the sun-drenched sky, Hugo retraced his steps to uncover Otto's opening. His friend sat there, shaken but safe.

Together, the two moved toward the village as sunlight cut through the trees. Hugo told the story to his friend but changed the parts he wished to remain secret. How could he possibly admit the killing would not stop?

Otto never questioned a single bit of the story.

In the end, Hugo returned to both the village and his family in Augsburg. At least, he would until signs of the beast took him, and he would become a danger to them. He did not know when, but soon enough uncontrollable urges would drive him into isolation to live off livestock or other creatures. Surely, humans would come for him someday. He knew it and dreaded the moment.

However, what truly tore him apart was the secret he had to keep from his children. His beloved Frieda and Hans—who always hugged him and begged him to play—knew nothing of the weight he carried. Hugo always obliged, without fail, because deep down, he understood that one day soon, he would be the one needing them, just as his father had once needed him.

Don't Touch the Artifacts

T revor rushed to the first aid station, leaving a spotted, meandering trail of blood behind him. Slamming his shoulder into the door, he forced it wide and bolted to the sink with shaky hands. One twist and warm water spouted from the faucet, coating his wound. Grimacing at the sting of pain shooting through his arm, he cursed himself for being careless with his newfound curiosity.

"How did this happen? There isn't a sharp edge on the thing, except for the stupid little spear the figure holds."

Being a Museum Technician, Trevor handled many artifacts every week—Mayan, Aztec, Sumerian, Egyptian, and more. But this one was different. No one, not from his staff or others worldwide, could place the piece to any culture. As such, Trevor believed it was akin to finding King Arthur's sword.

This unexplained piece appeared from nowhere, seemingly out of thin air, as the expression goes. Even after the staff viewed surveillance tapes, the piece's sudden arrival remained a mystery. One moment the idol was not there, then, as the video image glitched, the trinket was on the display shelf. Having the recording analyzed by an unending list of experts shed no light on the issue. There was no clear proof of tampering, leaving museum officials scratching their heads.

Still, it was a wonderfully ornate piece, and the curators chose to keep the artifact away from museumgoers' eyes until a deeper investigation could determine its origin.

Trevor had been carefully cleaning the piece, hoping to find an origin clue, when a stabbing pain ripped through his hand, slicing through his thin cotton gloves to leave a gash on his palm.

"It must have been the spear," he said, grabbing several paper towels to press against the wound.

Later, after a lengthy stay at the emergency room in which six stitches were threaded through the tender skin on his hand, Trevor headed home to rest. He felt lightheaded and weak. After feeding his fish and cats, he lay down and fell asleep in seconds.

———

The warm, cheerless night was dark, with a cloudless sky holding a new moon. Horrible dreams quickly haunted his rest. He tossed and turned as scantily clad natives wearing bizarre face paints pursued him through a jungle terrain he had never seen before. Mexico? Peru? Guatemala? He could not tell, nor did he care as he ran for his life. His breath came in ragged gasps, each step a desperate battle against the thick, choking jungle underbrush.

Branches whipped his face, stinging like fire, but he barely noticed. Behind him, the pounding of feet grew louder—faster. The natives were close.

Despite hours in the gym building stamina and strength, he

was no match for the fleet-footed, nimble natives who pursued him, weaving between trees like painted ghosts.

The scent of his sweat was thick in the humid air. Wholly outnumbered, he was caught in a deadly game of predator versus prey. In the end, he lost, knocked into a stupor as an accurately hurled rock struck his head with a sickening thud. The world spun, darkened, then collapsed into nothingness.

———

As his world came back into focus with a slow, sickening crawl, his head throbbed. Trying to move, pain shot through his neck. He discovered his wrists were bound, and his vision, still blurred, was enough to see several moving figures flickering in the dark gloom. They grew nearer.

In that moment, as a shrill shrieking sound reached his ears, he realized the terrible noise came from his own lips. Meanwhile, the natives danced round, cheering his torture, taking pleasure from his screams and pleas of mercy. Unfortunately, he received no quarter as they performed unimaginable acts of anguish to his bound form.

Hanging helplessly, tied harshly with barbed vines to wide stakes set some distance apart, they slashed at his tender skin with sharp knives and slowly relieved him of his fingers. And even when they wearied of their ways, the same could not be said of their anger. Instead, they sought new methods of torture, such as shooting arrows into his limbs or striking him with clubs.

Just when death loomed ever-closer, a tiny spark of understanding filled his mind. His captors were life-sized replicas of the statue from the museum in the waking world. Their facial paint, attire, tanned skin, and weapons were exact duplicates. Struggling to find the significance of his nightmares proved pointless as he lapsed into unconsciousness several times.

Once they threw icy water on his nakedness to wake him for the last dreadful design, his persecutors slowly peeled the skin from his body. Unable to endure a moment more, his overwhelmed, weakened body forced him from the nightmare, filling his cozy bedroom with screams.

Grabbing his comforter, Trevor pulled it to his chin and sobbed into his pillow, the pain seeming all too real as it wracked his quaking frame. He leapt up and dashed to the bathroom, fell on his knees and vomited, swearing to the gods between heaves he had done nothing wrong to deserve such a fate.

It's all in my imagination. A statue cannot bring such horrible dreams with it. I'm just tired and overworked.

Ambling back to his bed, he nearly stumbled over two furry lumps. His cats, Barnabas and Josette, hissed and leapt away from their sleeping spots to dash from the room.

"What! It's not like you haven't seen me sick before."

He crawled beneath the sheets and within minutes, sleep took him.

———

Trevor woke drenched in sweat. Sunlight poured through the curtains but offered no comfort. Every inch of his body throbbed with pain, as if his nightmares had carved themselves into his flesh.

As he sat up, the sheets fell away, revealing faint but unmistakable scratches across his arms and chest. They were too precise to be imagined and too real to ignore. He gingerly touched the red marks.

"Where the hell did those come from?"

He tried to remember last night. There had been more dreams, but that could not explain the vivid pain that woke him during slumber. It was too sharp. Even his cats, usually his loyal companions, avoided him, darting from the room as though sensing something he could not.

Unable to shake the unease, Trevor returned to the museum before opening hours, using his keycard to access the quiet, sterile halls. He did not turn on the lights. Instead, he made his way to the basement wing where the mysterious artifact was stored. Room 14B. Cabinet 3.

There it was: the same statue that had appeared inexplicably on the surveillance footage. Small, humanoid, and forged from materials that defied classification. Its pointed spear glinted behind the glass. Uncomfortable with the darkness, he flicked on the light and looked closer. The spear point caught his eye.

Is that blood?

He unlocked the case. The moment the glass swung open, a suffocating heat struck him. The overhead light flickered violently before going out altogether. *Damn the luck.*

Freeing his phone from his pocket, he aimed the flashlight at the statue. The beam faltered, then came steady but soft. As the light touched upon the figure's head, it shifted—tilting slightly, impossibly—toward him.

A petrified shriek wedged in his throat. Thoughts of fleeing filled his mind, but statue's presence pinned him, drawing him in. Then came the visions: a sky pierced by a black sun, temples carved into living rock, sacrifices moaning atop obsidian altars as they prepared for death, a civilization swallowed whole by something more ancient than time.

And at the heart of it all, this being. A forgotten god. Once worshiped, then sealed away to be erased from memory once the being turned spiteful and demanding. But now, it was angrier than ever before, hateful even. It wanted to be remembered, awakened.

The vision faded in a blink as Trevor collapsed onto the cold marble, gasping and twitching. The case had closed again, the statue silent and still. But its reflection in the glass door told another story.

Hazel eyes were rimmed in black. The irises were tinged a deep crimson. Veins pulsed visibly at his temples. Something ancient and wrathful had taken root inside.

———

Another sleepless night followed. This time, it was fear keeping Trevor awake. He stared at the ceiling, his body frozen beneath the weight of dread. Every corner of the room felt suffocating— a palpable, crushing pressure. Even as his eyelids grew heavy and his mind drifted toward sleep, the visions returned with brutal clarity.

Hopes of sleep vanished in a blink. He was no longer drifting into rest. He was falling into something dark, something alive.

Images of an irate god flooded in. A violent torrent of rage and pain consumed every thought, every fragment of his consciousness. The world faded away as the god's presence took shape within him, becoming vast, hollow, and terrifying.

Its voice rumbled, deeper than any human's, cold, yet so intimate it felt as if it had always been there, buried deep within him.

"You are my vessel to seek revenge."

The words were not his. He tried to claw back even a fragment of control, but his lips never moved. Neither his mind nor body was his any longer. The god's will was taking root, sinking deeper with each breath. Trevor was becoming the vessel.

Two days later, Trevor failed to report to work.

Surveillance footage showed him entering the museum basement early that Sunday morning—distracted, his movements jerky, uncoordinated—but he never came out. His coworkers reported nothing unusual, except for the odd stillness that settled over the building since his disappearance. The artifact remained. Untouched. Its case locked and undisturbed.

The glass case, perfectly maintained under the museum's climate controls, became clouded by condensation—thick mist curling against the surface as if the temperature inside had dropped sharply. But the controls had not shifted. The museum's climate expert swore it was impossible. Yet, there it was: the condensation, lingering like a silent omen.

And then there was the keycard. Trevor's keycard was found neatly placed within the artifact's case. It should not have been there, and no one could explain how it got inside, least of all the security team. They had repeatedly watched the footage and saw no sign of Trevor leaving.

In the following weeks, strange things began happening at the museum.

Staff members started reporting vivid dreams—nightmares of blood-soaked rituals, towering temples crumbling in the wake of a storm, and an ominous, looming presence that filled the sky like a dark sun. Their descriptions matched Trevor's accounts of the idol—its eyes, its form—but no one had truly believed him before. Now, they could not ignore it.

Curators who once dismissed Trevor's warnings as the ravings of an overworked, or perhaps an ill, mind, were just now understanding the horrifying truth. The artifact was not just a relic of the past; it was something far beyond their comprehension.

Trevor, in his desperation, had awakened it. But awakening it had cost him his humanity, and now, it had taken him entirely. The god was inside him, wrapped around his soul, clawing to the surface, demanding retribution.

No one ever knew where Trevor had gone or what had happened to him that day. But soon enough, the staff felt the intolerable pressure, the terror. Then in a monumental error, they opened the case.

Revenge

There were no clouds, yet the wind blew with fitful anger. In what seemed a sentient attempt to freeze my blood, the gusts forced themselves through my garments, unaffected by the numerous layers covering my person. Would there be no end to this night, I wondered as I trudged home, encouraged by the notion that safety and warmth would soon be mine.

Sadly, one of my first duties would be to burn my favorite suit and trousers. I sulked at the thought. I had paid a good deal of hard-earned money for them, and their loss saddened me. However, retaining them would prove folly, for their mere existence could easily prove my downfall. Losing fine clothing was an acceptable forfeiture, considering blood, fresh or dried, is dreadfully difficult to remove.

Pulling my collar tighter, I pushed harder against the swirling wind as I stepped onto the darkened path leading home. My chilled lips uttered a curse as, almost unwillingly, the memory of tonight's earlier event sprung forward.

To my horror, my lover suddenly appeared before my eyes

in dream-like fashion. Impossible! "You are a vision. You do not exist," I cried, knowing full well I had removed her from my life forever. Yet there she stood, wagging a finger and nagging, as was her usual, irksome way.

Why, I wondered. Why did she have to shout so? She had always cursed me, named me worthless, ranted over my habits concerning drink, labeling me overindulgent. The thread of her undoing unraveled completely once she disparaged my manliness, making vile references to things I would not stand for.

I argued in return, voicing my thoughts in a heated attempt to rationalize my consumption. I told her she had driven me to the bottle, which was a painful truth, but one I should never have spoken aloud. She grew angrier—then, unexpectedly, lashed out in a fury.

Setting aside her small stature, she fought like a demon—scratching, biting, and kicking with abandon. I labored to defend myself without doing her serious harm, but she persisted. Truly, it was not my intention to injure her, but in my drunken stupor, I struck her down as she assailed me for a third time. Should my conduct ever come to light, I will claim self-defense.

Admittedly, I should have walked away and spared her no more consideration before it came to that. Instead, separated from rational thought by means of rage, I seized a bookend and bludgeoned her. She buckled after the first blow, then collapsed in a heap with the second swing, but I did not stop until my strength was spent and she moved no more.

Exhausted, I slumped to the floor and stared at the horrid deed I had just done, but I remained still for no longer than a breath or two. Once my wits returned, I realized it was time to be rid of her forever. After heaving her lifeless form over my shoulder and beginning my trek into the woods, I learned that despite her diminutive size, she proved rather weighty. Using a shovel as a walking stick was helpful, and a stroke of genius, if I do say so. Forgive me, for I have strayed from the point.

Concerning the wretch's body in the present day, it is far underground. May the worms and maggots feast upon her hateful carcass. I ensured her vile, contemptuous voice would never ring in my ears again, nor would her loathsome hands ever touch me again. It must be said that her eternal silence brings me unbounded bliss.

Too, there is a calming comfort I take knowing she is not alone. The others are there, as well, buried beneath the cold, unfeeling dirt. There is a dark poetry of sorts binding them together. Completely unrelated, they became sisters in death, if you will. With eternity before them, perhaps they will come to love their earthly graves. Often, I have pondered if the dead even care about such things. Such was my mind as I reached my front door.

After a quick turn of the key, I pushed inside to hurriedly stoke the fire and bask in its warmth. Glancing over my cherished suit, I frowned as the smears of blood reflected in the flickering orange glow. Dashes of hope that it might yet be salvageable all but extinguished as the flames grew larger so I could look upon myself. I cursed the woman for forcing my unruly behavior.

Unable to endure the pungent odor of blood and sweat any longer, I drew a relaxing bath, then changed into sitting clothes. Moving to the fire once more, I tossed my ruined apparel into the flames, lingering there to watch them burn. They quickly transformed into gray ash before making a hasty escape up the chimney.

Satisfied, yet despondent over the loss of such fine material, I prepared a brandy, then eased into my overstuffed chair to ponder how my choice of past lovers had left me so empty. The last two years had witnessed nothing short of six female partners coming and going. That number alone gives one pause, no? None had proven themselves worthy of showing me lasting kindness or love. Thus, I ended my relationships in a way I deemed best: by silencing them forever.

I pondered if my existence would ever be improved by the presence of a female. Thus far, the answer is a resounding no. Yet I try, nonetheless. Perhaps it is foolish, but I have yet to let go of the hope that the right woman may ever be found.

Mind you, I do not consider myself a violent man but do admit my tolerance of insults is quite low. In hindsight, perhaps a few of my sweethearts did not deserve to be bludgeoned, stabbed, strangled, or tortured, but they refused to cease their pettiness or incessant nagging, regardless of my wishes to the contrary. What choice remained but to silence their infernal henpecking over my love of bottled spirits? Then or now, I see no other options.

Further, I argued, there was still the chance this entire scenario was little more than a figment of an overactive imagination. In my altered state, had I dreamt it all, or had I genuinely performed the evil deeds now weighing heavily on my consciousness?

I raised a shoulder to shrug away the idea, convinced the gods would refuse pity to those who had wronged me. Furthermore, I took satisfaction the women had already paid the ultimate price for their violations. I believed the miserable lot should indeed give recompence for what they forced me to do. Surely, if eternal damnation exists, it is now upon them. In any case, those women are nothing more than events from my past. Ones which I will consider no longer.

Fatigue, thanks in part to the day's strenuous events, had taken hold. With heavy eyes, I crossed the hardwood floors and found the creaking stairs. Minutes later, I snuggled into my warm bed, pulled the comforter tight, and closed my eyes.

Not long after, in the small hours of the night, a deafening bang jolted me awake. I sprang from bed wondering if I was trapped inside a Dickens novel alongside his fictional, cursed spirits. I half expected to see an apparition rattling chains or moaning as it drifted through my chambers. But there was none. Silence had fallen over the house.

Still, I seized my favorite walking stick from beside the dresser, then crept along the corridor and down the stairs, pausing now and again to grimace at their accursed squeaking. Even the stairs in my own sanctuary seemed alive, wishing to alert the intruder to my presence.

Noises unlike any I have ever heard wafted to my ears as I reached the first floor in the form of odd scratching, shuffling, and knocking. Had the gates of Hell swung wide and led its atrocities here to discover me? Had they come to claim me for my past acts? It was not the first time I pondered such questions.

I followed the sounds which grew in frequency, my stick held at the ready with both hands. Save for the glowing embers of the night's fire and slivers of pale moonlight shining through windows, the house was horribly dark, but lighting a lantern would need to wait. I would not release my weapon to strike a match.

Twice I stumbled forward as my bare toes impacted a chair or table leg. I stifled several curses and pressed on, regardless of the shooting pain. If what I thought could be awaiting me was indeed here, this pain would soon be the least of my concerns.

So it was, I reached the confines of my sitting room where I met an unexpected sight. Seated in my chair was a shapely figure touched upon by the moonbeams. Clearly a woman, yet I could see little around her through the suffocating blackness. I paused. Was she alone or need I watch for her partner, or partners, to accost me from the shadows?

Moving stealthily, never taking my eyes from her for no more than a blink, I edged toward the hearth. Slowly navigating to the far right of my sitting chair, ottoman, and end table, I tossed kindling upon the dying fire to add more light. The flames sprang to life in an instant. Dozens of glowing embers floated about in a shower of tiny orange orbs as they raced up the flue and onto the floor.

As the orangish glow spread over the room, my gaze settled on the trespasser and at once doubt claimed my sanity. Before me, with eyes paler than parchment and fresh dirt covering her clothing and face, sat Mary, the woman I had buried not twelve hours ago. Impossible, I shouted for the second time this day.

With hands neatly folded in her lap, she stared forward, motionless, seemingly ignoring my presence. Dried blood matted her hair, and deep lacerations lined her scalp from the bludgeoning she had received. Her skull was sunken on one side. She was a ghastly sight. I pressed my hand against my lips and backed away.

How? How is she here? Could she see me as I saw her? Mayhap the dead cannot speak to the living. Then, a question most foul entered my mind. Was she dead, completely and utterly? Had she somehow survived to claw her way free from her grave to return and haunt me? Perchance, she truly is dead but believes herself still amongst the living. That I hoped was true, for otherwise I was trapped in a twisted dream from which I must escape.

Before, I was sure of her state of being. Now, though I called her name softly, she continued to present no movement nor acknowledge my existence. Nary a twitch was seen, nor a sound heard, though I spoke her name several more times, each one louder than the last. Why will this repulsive vision not acknowledge me? My feet shifted nervously beneath me while those awful, unblinking white eyes stared ahead.

I edged closer, unknowingly tightening my fingers round my stick until feeling was lost. Each moment became agony as doubts over my earlier handiwork resurfaced. Mary cannot still draw breath, can she? Mayhap she returned to seek an apology. Worse still, had she forgiven my rash deed and returned to me in ghostly form? No! I shook my head, vainly attempting to do away with such foolhardy thoughts. Moments of insanity were all they were. No, I repeated. I had removed her from my life, as surely as I breathed air.

The banging returned, this time from behind. I twisted round to meet yet another figure staring blankly, causing me to gasp as I met her whitened gaze. "It cannot be," I shouted.

Antionette stood before me with outstretched arms. Whether to hold me in a loving embrace within her long ashen limbs or put me to death by means of an unnatural touch, I shuddered to think. Nor did I wish to know. I swooned in fear and backed away from the hearth, past the chair, keeping distance by means of my walking stick.

Unlike Mary, Antionette drew closer, allowing the firelight to shine upon her once-lovely face. The dancing color gruesomely highlighted the neat incision running the width of her neck, and even as I retreated, I could not escape the memory of her untimely death.

After a particularly nasty disagreement, I had had enough. I slunk into the shadows of the house to wait, then sprang upon her as she passed. From behind, I grasped her hair and yanked back hard to expose her soft neck. Following a swift sideways motion, the deed was done. She fell in a spasming heap, gurgling gruesome sounds as one hand clutched the wound in a futile attempt to halt the bleeding. Meanwhile, the other reached out in a pointless gesture of begging for help. As if I could—or wished to—make it stop.

That was her price for being unfaithful, thereby insulting

my personal pride on several levels. My final act against her was to stand witness as the life spark drained from her eyes, leaving them dull and unblinking as they were now.

Eight months ago, I buried her, my fifth lover, amongst the flora and tall trees, there in the circle with the others. Like Mary, she, too, had most certainly been dead as I covered her with cold earth. Yet now she was here, still moving like a phantom gliding across the floor. How, I pondered with rising desperation, could I wake myself from his nightmare?

Another bang, and another, and another, and another rose up. The accursed sounds were deafening, like an otherworldly door opening, then slamming shut as wicked spirits entered the realm of the living. The mere thought made me wail as, one by one, they assembled.

Now, here in my sanctum sanctorum, I faced them all. Mary, Sarah, Charlotte, Josephine, Antoinette, and Margaret. They drew nearer, their vile white eyes boring into me, driving me closer to madness. Their pallid skin nearly glowed in the dark.

With every drifting step, their circle tightened. Trapped, I lashed out with my cane. The shaft impacted Sarah's head with force but, to my disbelief, did nothing to slow her. Instead, she hissed like an angry cat as her feet slapped the hardwood floor with an indescribable, sickening sound. Her advance continued.

With no other option, I rushed ahead, attempting to force myself between Charlotte and Mary. As I did, my agonized screams rent the air as Josephine lunged to rip at my skin with unnaturally long nails. My thigh turned warm and moist as crimson liquid flowed into my slipper. Wholly unnerved, I lost my wits and stumbled in the dark, landing on all fours. My walking stick skittered from sight to disappear in the room's deep blackness as another brutal lash opened an ever-deeper wound on my bicep. Coursing pain and adrenaline surged through my vulnerable form, and in the next moment, I lost all reason. Swiping blindly around me, I cleared a brief opening in the hideous circle and sprang up.

I hobbled to my bed chamber, slamming and bolting the door behind me before frantically rummaging through my closet for a cloth to staunch the bleeding. Tearing loose two long shirtsleeves, I wrapped the wounds as best I could with shaking hands. Only when they were sufficiently bandaged did my foolish, inadvertent decision come to light—there was no egress from the second floor, save the staircase by which I arrived. Once again, I was trapped.

From the hallway rose the horrible slapping sound of corpses' cold feet as my victims drew ever nearer. Covering both ears with my hands, I huddled in a corner, sank to the floor, and screamed as their shrill voices raised up in a bizarre chorus of hate and revenge. The sound was akin to a fabled banshee, one who wails or screeches to herald death. With all of them gathered tonight and my blood soaking rapidly through the cloth, I could wholly believe my former lovers were heralding my demise.

My long-hidden worries scattered as the banging returned. This time, it was pounding upon my chamber door. I cursed my choice of concealment.

Doomed I would be, should the door give way to the dead. Wounds still bleeding freely, I feared I could not overpower the six specters plaguing me. Dizziness and panic wormed deeper into my brain. Then, in a sudden burst of clear thought, I recalled the hidden passage behind the bookcase. Its path led to the sitting room. From there, I could escape by means of the front door.

Pain ripped my body as I fought to stand. One hand outstretched to steady myself against the night table, I spared a quick glance and fought down the rising bile at the sight. My leg wound had worsened considerably, turning black and spreading up my thigh, burning as it coursed through my veins and covered my skin. My arm was in a similar state. The agony was mind-numbing.

I limped to the mantle, worked the lever, struggled greatly to light the hanging lantern, then hobbled into the musty darkness. Closing the door on the continued wailing, I snuck along as quietly as able, focusing solely on the forced breaths rattling in and out of my chest. Before long, I exited into the den with a sigh of relief. Collecting my wits, I hurried to the front entry, flung it open, and dashed into the night. Fright overtook pain, adding speed to my uneven steps.

The shrieking behind me lessened again, yet it brought little relief. Sweat beaded my brow as I held my lantern low and tottered down the winding trail. Surely, my neighbors would be home. Shelter and aid would be found amongst them, I thought. They were gentle folk and would not turn me away unless they knew what was hunting me. Gritting my teeth to stop the moans, I vowed to refrain from uttering a word of the death-bearing creatures lest they shunned me for fear of their own safety.

Farther on, from between the branches of the gently swaying trees, came a dim light. Hope sprang into my heart. Each footfall brought me closer to it, yet to my horror, the haunting voices followed, echoing louder. My escape had been discovered.

Then, in a moment beyond all reasoning or understanding, another bang ran out. Without warning, Charlotte blocked my way. She still wore her most cherished scarf, the one I tightly wrapped round her neck to choke away her last breath. The atrocious piece of cloth still disgusted me as my eyes settled on her. In life, despite my teasing ridicule of the thing, she wore the horrid piece to annoy me. It was only fitting, then, that I made it the instrument of her demise.

Rattled to my core, I could stand no more. I screamed at her to let me be, wailing that she was no longer amongst the living and demanded she leave me in peace. But as was her way when alive, she disregarded my words.

In a blink she covered the distance to stand mere inches before me, arm raised to slash at my face. Weak and wobbly as I was, defense seemed nigh impossible. I raised an arm only to have her claw-like fingers rip another deep gash through my skin. I cried out and stumbled. The world around me turned indistinct.

Backing away as the new laceration ran stingingly fresh with blood, I swung my lantern wildly in hopes of defense. It brought no relief, nor did it gain me advantage, save placing distance between us. Then, the banging resumed as others stepped from the night's depths into my lantern's wavering light.

Their speed was overwhelming. Sarah came next, swiping her sharp, talon-like nails at my flesh. I knew it was her for I recognized the small, key-shaped birthmark on her neck, the blemish that, to me, marred her beauty in totality. She was perfect in all other physical aspects, but the mark made her much less so. Unable to view the disfigurement even as I bled out, I lurched away.

The move proved a mistake, for I was struck hard about the head. More blood ran over my shoulder as something soft, almost mushy, landed between my feet. Vomit broke from my lips as I gawked at the fleshy appendage of my ear, which came to a final rest atop my slipper.

I stood frozen, as did the women, staring at me with brutal satisfaction. Moments passed with no words spoken before the terrors fell upon me once more, slashing with their long nails, bludgeoning me with rocks, or biting deep with pointed teeth. My eyesight dimmed. Darkness crept in, solidifying as if it knew it could no longer be stopped.

Then, in a moment of shock that rivaled my reunion with all my former lovers, all hurt and despair abandoned me and I was left with a sense of remarkable calm. Oddly, my thoughts turned to a scientific theory I had once read, how the mind protects the body from intolerable pain by removing all sensations from nerve endings.

I had scoffed then, but now, as I lay unfeeling, unable to move as they exacted their revenge, I deem there is a great deal of truth in it. My body jerked to and fro as they brutalized my form. My final thought as death closed in was how the experience was cold, lonely, and miserable. As I grew detached from my mortal body, another chilled realization took me.

Never again would I witness things I once held dear—a sunrise, birds taking flight, or the aroma of a rainy spring day. My life was all for naught, and that fact will haunt me until time is no more.

With all its faults, this cruel death shall be *my* payment for past indiscretions.

In these final moments I hold great remorse for what I have done, including the copious amount of drink that placed me in such a pitiful state, though I firmly believe I do not deserve such a heinous ending as this. In various forms, these women attempted to staunch my drinking, debased me, and drove me to my actions. For that, I should not need suffer such a cruel fate as I do now.

Just know that murder, a deed so foul one can hardly imagine the toll it takes on one's soul, came far too easily in each of my cases. I wonder if anyone will truly miss the wretches or place blame upon me for dispatching those who caused such injustice to my heart and mind? I think not.

Yet it is not my decision what is right or wrong. The gods will choose that portion of my destiny and suffering for me.

Now, I conclude each of us shall be held accountable for this life's actions and pay in one form or another, even for behaviors we believe to be the best course at the time. So if not answerable in this world, I will undoubtedly pay in the next, wherever that may be.

Farewell, cruel and unjust world.

The Monsters of Grimhaven

E very year, on All Hallow's Eve, as the veil between the living and the dead thinned, something dark slithered through the streets of Grimhaven. It was thick with malevolent energy. And in the shadows, where the old trees creaked and groaned, the monsters came out to play.

Grimhaven was no ordinary town. Here, the children—both brave and foolish alike—didn't just wander the safe streets. No, they ventured beyond, into the hills, forests, and homes of the things that should not exist.

For centuries, the town had lived under an unspoken pact, a dark agreement made long ago between the town and the monsters dwelling just beyond the borders. The monsters were granted permission to indulge their whims, but they were bound within the confines of their homes, their caves, their lairs in the hills. They could have their fun, their tricks, but Grimhaven itself was off-limits. Though the monsters' appetites were vast, they respected the boundaries. But like anything, it came with a price.

Some believed it was a curse, a consequence of something

the townsfolk had done long ago. Others thought it was a deal, struck in desperation to secure human survival. Either way, it was a truth no one dared question.

Every year, children would disappear, swept away by those who lived just out of sight and beyond our suppressed knowledge.

As always, the high-pitched screams of the boys and girls—small, fleeting things—were swallowed whole by the mist. No doubt, an unquestioned price for foolishness. The cost of trespass, paid in fear and silence.

———

This year began as any other—children filled the streets in colorful costumes, each one excited to get more candy than their siblings or friends. The usual suspects paraded as witches, ghosts, and superheroes. But a few of the older kids, brimming with the naive courage only youth could afford, began to whisper about Old Man Kraven.

"Did you hear? He gives out full-size bars," Sarah said with a sly grin, her crooked witch's hat slipping to one side. "He lives in the hills. That's where the real candy's at."

Jake hesitated, his plastic Dracula hair and fake vampire fangs gleaming in the streetlight. "Hold up! You know as well as I do, no one ever comes back from the hills after dark. They say Kraven's a werewolf, and after sundown—"

"—no one comes back." Sarah scoffed, before her eyes lit up with challenge. "That's why it's going to be legendary. Just you and me, Jake. We'll knock on Kraven's door, get the candy, and be back before anyone notices. We'll be heroes. Famous, even. Besides, do you really believe he is a werewolf?"

Jake looked unsure. But Sarah's grin was contagious, and the lure of fame and bragging rights was impossible to ignore.

———

By the time they reached Old Man Kraven's mansion, the fog had thickened, swirling around their ankles like a sentient being. The house loomed before them, towering and oppressive, its stone walls darkened by the years and the forest's suffocating embrace. A single lantern flickered dimly behind the fog, casting ghostly shadows on the windows.

Jake glanced up, swallowing hard. "I don't know, Sarah. This doesn't feel right."

"Come on, dude. That's nonsense." Sarah clucked like a chicken, then chuckled and turned to the house. Jake followed slowly.

Taking a deep breath, she knocked on the door three times, each louder than the last. The sound echoed, deep and hollow, like a bell tolling for the dead.

For a moment, silence. Then a low growl rumbled from the other side, followed by a series of sniffing sounds—slow and deliberate.

The door creaked open. Old Man Kraven stood tall in the doorway. His fur glistened in the moonlight, his eyes gleaming like molten gold, predatory and cold. His grin stretched wide, revealing teeth too sharp for any human to possess.

"Trick or treat?" His voice was smooth like the sky with no visible stars. Pure darkness itself.

Sarah held out her plastic pumpkin. It was shaking in her trembling hands. "Trick or treat!" she echoed, her voice a little too high-pitched.

Kraven's eyes flicked to the basket, then back to her. His smile widened, the hunger in his gaze unmistakable. "Well, well... treats are for fools." His voice dripped with malice. "I think it's time for a trick."

Before Sarah could react, his clawed hand shot out, grabbing her wrist with a speed that made Jake flinch. Kraven's talons dug deep into her skin, releasing a thin trail of blood. She gasped in shock, her wide eyes pleading.

"Stop! Let her go!" Jake shouted, his bravado crumbling in the face of terror.

The beast's laughter was low as he yanked Sarah inside with terrifying strength. Her scream cut through the night but was quickly muffled as the door slammed shut.

Jake stood frozen. He soiled himself as a scream tore up from his throat. But no sound came. Paralyzed by fear, his feet refused to move.

In a blink, Kraven reappeared in the doorway, his hands covered in fresh blood. His grin was wild, as if he had just enjoyed a most delicious treat.

"Mmmm..." he hummed, his voice thick with satisfaction. "I smell fear. And you, my boy, smell like dessert."

Kraven licked his lips slowly, his gaze locking on Jake. "No one will ever miss you, little vampire."

Panic surged through Jake, breaking his paralysis. He spun on his heels and ran as the fog twisted around him, disorienting him, trapping him. The gnarled, ancient trees seemed to reach for him, their limbs grasping at his clothing. He cursed Sarah and her impulsiveness for bringing him here.

Behind him, Kraven howled, a sound that made his blood run cold. It was a signal—a call to the pack. From the darkness, a dozen glowing eyes appeared.

Wolves, monstrous, massive beasts, their jaws gleaming with hunger, moved with terrifying speed. Jake knew they would catch him before he could escape. Tears of hopelessness flowed over his cheeks.

———

The next morning, the streets of Grimhaven were alive with children, laughing and playing, their bags full of candy. But there was emptiness, too. An uneasy quiet lay thick over the town.

Jake and Sarah were missing, just like so many before them. The town went on, oblivious to the price that had been paid.

And yet, as the townsfolk would prepare for another Halloween, the monsters knew it had been a good year. The bravest, the boldest, had ventured into the hills, thinking themselves invincible. But the monsters were always hungry, and the game was never really about candy.

It was about survival.

———

This day, once the children returned from their play, a strange thing happened. A boy named Danny, small and inquisitive, sat alone on the curb, his bag of candy forgotten beside him. He had been too scared to participate in the adventure this year, but something was missing, gnawing at him as his eyes flicked over the emptying streets.

In the distance, he saw a figure standing on the hill, watching from the shadows. It was the legendary Kraven. Or at least, someone who looked like him.

Danny stood, drawn by an unfamiliar compulsion. The figure's eyes glinted as he beckoned the young lad toward him.

"Come, boy. I still have plenty of candy," Kraven's voice called. "You've been waiting for this."

And as Danny crossed the street, the fog closed in around him, and he knew the monsters had always been part of the game. But they were breaking the rules. Halloween was over . . . at least for some.

After all, some treats are too hard to pass up.

The Fall of Humanity

Once, the city thrived with the hum of modern life: traffic snarls, buzzing smartphones, gleaming glass, and watchful drones flying high overhead. Before, I was an animal rights activist and attorney for several companies trying to bring deplorable animal testing to a close. Those days felt like another lifetime.

Now, the skyline, previously towering and sleek, has been overtaken by rust and decay. Skyscrapers, once viewed as symbols of man's achievements, stand stripped of their former glory, little more than hollow skeletons with ivy-covered, cracked foundations.

Save for the occasional tapping of claws on pavement, the streets are eerily quiet—especially at night. Humans rarely venture out anymore, and never after curfew. There is no need. Plus, it is against the rules. Rules made by animals—many of the same we routinely slaughtered for meat.

That is, until they had had enough. Now, they are no longer the animals we once knew. These creatures walk upright, their eyes gleaming with intelligence, their voices eerily human, as though they have been waiting for this moment, listening for ages to finally reclaim their place in the world.

We first saw them at the zoo. Everything seemed so ordinary then. It was not supposed to be a takeover. We had watched them in their cages—chimpanzees, lions, wolves, and birds—staring back as we gawked, teased, and ruled them, often by harsh, violent means that went unspoken. Some, like me, tried to protect the animals, but so few were their number that they made little difference.

All that changed once the animals began to speak.

———

It was a late summer evening when the animals started to move, just after the sun dipped below the horizon. A strange calm swept over the city. People had been sitting in their cars, waiting in traffic to rush home to their mundane, boring lives, when they saw the first one: a large wolf, towering seven feet, standing in an intersection. Its fur was thick, a blend of silvery grays, deep browns, and streaks of white that reflected the light, and its eyes gleamed an unnatural gold. Then came the voices, primal and hoarse but bearing an unmistakable message.

"Our time has come. The Reckoning has arrived."

A few curious drivers stepped out to stare at the beast, unsure if it was real or a hallucination. Then some turned violent, grabbing for their guns and trying to do what man always does to things they cannot understand or accept—destroy it.

Yet the animals were prepared. After all, they had thousands of years to anticipate this day. They knew that violence and death is all we know, so as the humans raised their guns, they were struck down without mercy—just as our race had done to the animals for countless generations.

One particularly ignorant fellow, his shiny gun trained on the wolf leader, was snatched from his shoes by an enraged elephant. The large bull repeatedly smashed the squealing man against the pavement until he was little more than a bloodstain on the road. Other gun-toting humans quickly met the same fate, as well.

After that, the takeover was swift. The zoo, which reported a breakout earlier in the day, was now abandoned and left to rot. It has become a breeding ground and headquarters of sorts —a sanctuary, if needed.

Within days, gorillas, tigers, hawks, macaws, and even monkeys appeared on street corners, standing tall, their postures regal and proud. City residents, confused and horribly frightened, scattered into their homes, closing windows and locking doors as if thin glass and wood would keep them safe.

The first few weeks were a surreal nightmare. There was no real fight. No mass attempt at resistance, no heroes. We were reduced to mere subjects in their reign, forced to adapt and shell-shocked after what seemed like an overnight upheaval—subtle at first, like an infestation no one saw coming. In the beginning, the creatures did not kill unless threatened. But within weeks, there were no lengths they would not go to even the score. In this world, for every animal a human killed, twenty humans would die in their place as retribution. Within two months, terrified people could only obey—at least, if they wished to stay alive.

Of course, there were subversive human groups, of which I belonged to three. But we quickly realized attempts at resistance brought threefold destruction. Opposition in any form was severely punished.

For a time, I bordered on insanity. Being locked away in my apartment with no free will nearly drove me over the edge. There were no more shopping trips, no more friends, no more living a 'normal' life. We exist to serve them. Still, I survive, all while trying to piece together a new life in a world ruled by those who demand total submission, just as we had done to them.

My name is Kate, and I'm one of the few who still reflect on what we could've and should've done differently to prevent ruining everything we touch. But in the end, my thoughts are too little, too late—the exact obstacle of the human race.

I currently live in what used to be a high-rise apartment building. Now, it's more like a prison, though nobody dares call it that. The air reeks of decay, blood, and death.

Occasionally, an animal passes by, sniffing at the garbage bags that line the streets. I've had a few close calls with the beasts. Once, a cheetah came by, with its alert eyes gazing through my window. I didn't know if she could sense my fear or if she was simply curious. Perhaps she viewed me as a snack. Either way, the encounter was enough to make me stay still until I heard her paws retreat into the distance.

But then *she* came.

I had never seen a creature like her before. The first time I laid eyes upon her, I thought she was a vision. The Doe. A tall, slender creature with fur the color of lightly toasted bread and eyes so dark they could have belonged to a human. She stood across the street watching everything with an eerie calm. She was incredibly beautiful in an unsettling way—delicate yet powerful, as though she could end your existence with a single graceful movement.

I watched from the safety of my apartment window. She

bore the same regal posture as the others, but her demeanor was clearly different. She was more fluid, more deliberate, like that of a queen trained in the art of poise and grace.

She didn't seem like the type who would simply demand compliance like the wolves, tigers, or bears. No, she possessed more intellect. There was an undeniable quiet strength about her, a knowing.

For days, she returned to stand by the apartment entrance, her eyes ever-vigilant as they swept over the broken city. Her vigilance never faltered. Her attention never turned toward the humans huddled in their homes. Oddly, it felt as if she was waiting for me—though I couldn't understand why.

Truthfully, I felt sorry for her and understood her in some small ways. To be hunted and killed at the whim of humans must have been simply awful. Empathy crept into my heart, but it never quite silenced the fear I was learning to live with.

Through her daily visits, it wasn't long before I noticed a pattern. She would appear every evening at the same time, silent, unmoving for hours. She rarely approached the others directly, unless it was to issue orders. Otherwise, she merely watched.

Curiosity bit at me. I needed to know more about her—what she wanted, what her presence meant in a world that had spiraled into chaos from our own inhumanity. There was no one to blame but ourselves.

Even now—a retribution for past deeds, as I overheard one cow say—the animals round us up weekly, forcing us to fight to the death, just as our twisted society once made dogs, roosters, and countless other innocent creatures suffer the same fate.

They lock the selected ones in tiny cages as we did to pigs, chickens, and more, then spray the confused, begging humans with powerful fire hoses. They offer no mercy, no relief, until the captives' final time comes. For no reason, they hit them with boards, pipes, hammers, or whatever is handy. They shock the selected ones with cattle prods and ask how it feels to be help-less and tortured for no reason. Animals experiment on the Selected as we did to rabbits and many sentient beings.

Many of the large cats keep their instincts sharp by hunting the Selected for meat. After all, they must eat, too, right?

One main rule was simple enough: humans were disal-lowed from breeding.

Why anyone would wish to bring a child into this world befuddled me, but I suppose some people are simply born stupid.

With that in mind, I decided to take a risk. What is the worst that can happen, I wondered. Would the Doe kill me, or have me killed? Perhaps that is best anyway. I want desperately to live, but the loss of hope has a disturbing effect on one's mind. I hoped she would listen to a semblance of reason.

Making my way downstairs one night when the air felt cooler, a rare relief in the stifling city, I noticed the streets were empty. It was nearly curfew, and I did not have long.

From today's rain, the air smelled of wet concrete and old trash. I approached the entrance, where the Doe stood in her usual spot.

As I neared, her eyes flicked toward me, but she remained motionless. Her gaze was intense, yet not aggressive. For a moment, I froze, unsure and terrified of what to do. Then, as if reading my thoughts, she spoke.

"You are different. Tell me: why are you here?" Her voice had a sharp edge, yet compassion and curiosity were there, too.

I was not expecting her to engage. Truthfully, I'm not sure what I was expecting. Death? Anger? Hatred? Perhaps all three. She had that right, I suppose.

My first thought was questioning whether I could trust her. The second, a concern over whether she was speaking to me. I glanced around. We were alone. I suppose that answers that question.

She took a slow step toward me, and I instinctively stepped back. She stopped.

"What do you want from us?" I managed to ask, my voice barely a whisper. "How can humans restore themselves in your eyes?"

Her eyes darkened as an odd connection formed between us. Almost as if her thoughts were clear to me.

"The question is not what *I* want," she replied. "It is what *you* want. And your filthy kind will never hold status in this world again. You have abused animals and this planet—our home—for quite long enough. Earth has never needed your kind. You are a plague to our existence."

I frowned, confused. "What are you saying? That's not true. There are good people all around you. Ones you sentence to death without reason."

The Doe snorted and stomped a hoof on the ground in protest. "Before you led us into slaughter pens by the millions, did you ever ask if we wanted to die simply to feed your hunger? No! Not once, not ever. We only wanted peace, an even share of love and affection with your kind. Your only response was inventing new ways to kill us for the sake of your endless appetites."

My eyes widened. "I fought for animals. It was my job. I tried to save you all."

The Doe's eyes settled on me, warm and soft for an instant. "*That* is the only reason you are still alive, Kate Morton. We know of you and for your kindness toward us, you shall remain alive until your body expires."

I initially wanted to take back what humans believe is theirs—the world. But then, the Doe's words made perfect sense. This takeover was simply what the planet needed and wanted. The big blue marble never needed humanity. Never needed me.

So now that the time has come for me to plea humanity's case, I chose not to. I accepted what has happened and will fight no more. Humanity caused its own downfall, and I was the last nail in the coffin, their final hope.

"I understand," I said weakly. "For what it's worth, I am sorry."

"We often wondered how humans live with themselves. Your kind is pathetic. Even now as you are conquered, you fight amongst yourselves, thinking you can win or somehow prolong your ever-violent existence. But it is already decided. You will submit. The forest has called to us. Mother Earth and her original inhabitants are reclaiming their world. This is our time. For your past deeds, you will know what it is like to be subjugated, made to kill one another, to be a food source, and to never know love again until the end of time."

I swallowed, my thoughts racing. "And what do you want from me?"

Her lips curled into the faintest of smiles. "You've made it this far. You see. You understand. But you cannot stop it. You can choose to submit and live in peace or resist and be swept away."

I wanted to shout, to tell her that I'd never submit, that I'd fight until my last breath. That is what my race does. But when I opened my mouth, the words formed a horrible taste I could not ignore.

The humiliation of what we have done to animals surfaced like a submarine breeching the water's surface. The suffocating stillness of the moment pressed in on me. I felt lightheaded.

I took another shaky step back and her gaze softened again. There was sympathy in her expression. "You shall make your choice soon enough," she murmured before fading into the shadows.

———

The following days were worse than before. If possible, the city's streets grew quieter, the windows of buildings more tightly shut. The animals, ever present, still prowled the shadows, watching with eyes that see all.

Some folks still tried to organize, to resist, but each time they attempted to reclaim what we'd lost, the animals met them with overwhelming force. They kept their promise of killing us by the score if a single animal was harmed.

They broke us down piece by piece. People trying to rise against them eventually fell to their knees in compliance or died violently in the end.

I haven't seen her since that night, but I know she's out there, waiting with the patience of a clam.

I have accepted the fact that animals rule now. We no longer control the world. And as I sit here, in the ruins of a once-great city, I realize one horrifying truth: they were right. The forest is calling, and the land is indeed reclaiming its own. The Kingdom of Fur, as we named it, is here to stay.

We humans are but the last remnants of a dying species. And before we perish from history, we will pay for the intolerable crimes of all those who came before us, of all those—ourselves included—who gave little thought to what we have done to those with whom we share this world.

Afterword

The Last Gasping Breath

You made it to the end. Not everyone does.

Dear Reader,

Thank you for daring to step into the dark. These stories were stitched together from shadow, memory, and things better left unnamed. But you read them anyway.

If the stories made your skin crawl, made your heart race, or left you checking the locks twice . . . consider leaving a review. Your words could pull others into the dark . . . or warn them to stay away.

A short review on Amazon, Goodreads, or wherever you got this book helps summon new readers into the darkness and keeps the stories alive.

And if you'd like to know what else lurks in the corners of my mind, you can find me at Next Journey Books. (www.nextjourneybooks.com)

Afterword

Sleep well, if you can.

Mark K. McClain